Interior Design by Christina Smith

Books By Natasha Madison

The Only One Series
Only One Kiss
Only One Chance
Only One Night
Only One Touch
Only One Regret
Only One Moment
Only One Love
Only One Forever

Southern Series
Southern Chance
Southern Comfort
Southern Storm
Southern Sunrise
Southern Heart
Southern Heat
Southern Secrets
Southern Sunshine

This Is
This is Crazy
This Is Wild
This Is Love
This Is Forever

Hollywood Royalty
Hollywood Playboy
Hollywood Princess
Hollywood Prince

Something So Series
Something Series
Something So Right
Something So Perfect
Something So Irresistible
Something So Unscripted
Something So BOX SET

Tempt Series
Tempt The Boss
Tempt The Playboy
Tempt The Ex
Tempt The Hookup
Heaven & Hell Series
Hell And Back
Pieces Of Heaven

Love Series
Perfect Love Story
Unexpected Love Story
Broken Love Story

Faux Pas
Mixed Up Love
Until Brandon

Dedication

Matteo you are a force to be reckoned with.
I'm so proud of the boy you were and the man you are becoming.

Don't let anything or anyone stop you!

Someday when the pages of my life end,
I know that you will be one of the most beautiful chapters.
Anonymous

Southern Secrets

Amelia

Never make the same mistake twice is my motto.
After being left in the dust of an old pickup truck, I
promised that I would take care of myself and never trust
another man with a sexy smirk and cowboy boots.
Then he showed up, and he's everywhere I turn, making
me want something I shouldn't.

Asher

I grew up in foster care, and on my eighteenth birthday,
I was set free.
I spent years coasting from town to town.
Staying wasn't a part of my plan and neither was love,
but somehow, I found both.
This was all supposed to be temporary. I'm hoping my
secret doesn't destroy the only family I've ever known.

Southern secrets

One

Asher

"ADMIT IT." I turn around to see Amelia on her horse trotting toward me. Her blond hair bounces up and down as she trots over.

"Admit what?" I ask. I ignore the pull in my stomach when I turn and see her smiling. And not the fake smile she usually gives people. This smile lights up her whole face, making her eyes squint even more. I've been around for the past six months, and it's a smile I've tried to see on her face every day. I get off the horse and take him by the reins. The sun shines high in the sky with not a cloud in sight.

"You *should* be better than me." I wait for her to get beside me. "You've been riding for your whole life." I chuckle. "I've been riding for six months." Before coming to this town, all I knew how to do was odd jobs here and there. Usually bussing tables or working in the kitchen, now what started out as mucking stalls turned into me making sure all the barns had everything they needed to run.

"Don't make excuses," she says as she walks beside me, both of us holding on to the reins of our horses as they walk leisurely beside us. "You said you would smoke me and you didn't." She repeats the words I stupidly said last week when she beat me. "Just say it." She has to be the most competitive person that I know. She can never lose and if she does she just comes back even harder.

We walk into the barn side by side. I place the horse in his stall while I watch Amelia make her way over with her horse to her stall. I watch her for a second longer than I should before turning my head and going to get water.

"So are you going to say it?"

Looking over my shoulder, I find Amelia leaning against the barn stall, dressed in her blue jeans, plaid shirt, and cowboy boots. She arrived with her blond hair loose, but once she saddled her horse, she piled it on top of her head. "What do you want me to say, Amelia?" I fold my arms over my chest. Ever since I came into town, she's always ready to spar with me. We play this cat and mouse game, unsure of how the other one feels.

"Just say I'm better than you." She smirks at me, and when I glare at her, she claps her hands together and lets out a howling laugh. I want to march over to her and kiss the ever-loving shit out of her, but instead, I remind myself of what a bad fucking idea that is.

"I'd rather eat crow." I force myself to turn instead of staring at her and watching her laugh. I shake my head as I mouth, "Eat crow? What the fuck?" It shows I've been here longer than any other place if I'm starting to repeat phrases like that.

"Come on," she says softly. "It's time to eat." I look over at her. "You always get grouchy when you go two hours without eating."

"I do not." I glare at her. Why do I let her get under my skin? It's her turn to fold her arms over her chest. We spend most mornings together and then half of the afternoon on the phone, so it's no wonder she knows things about me.

"When was the last time you ate?" she asks, and I walk right past her. The sound of her chuckling makes my skin heat.

She jogs to catch up to me. "You usually have a snack at around ten." She keeps up with my long strides.

I stop. "You watching me?" I tilt my head to the side. "That is kind of stalkerish, don't you think?" I tease, and I want to reach up and curl the strand of hair that has fallen out of her tied hair.

She opens her mouth and closes it again. "Don't flatter yourself, Asher," she huffs out, turning to stomp away.

As I watch her walk away, Reed and his best friend, Christopher, come up behind me. "She smoked you good," Reed says, dressed in Levi's and a plaid shirt with his worn cowboy boots. He's the only one who wears a cowboy hat every Sunday. Reed slaps me on the shoulder, laughing as he walks past me to the food.

Looking around, I'm blown away at how big this barbecue is. Every Sunday, the same people come, yet there are always new faces. I put my head down and walk over to the food table. "Hey." I look up when I hear Ethan walking toward me. "You look like someone stole your dog."

I shake my head as we walk to the table of food. "Just thinking about the things I have to do tonight."

"You know you can take Sunday off," he says. "There is nothing you do on Sunday that can't wait until Monday morning."

"I know," I say. "But I have nothing else to do." I stop talking when we get in line for the food. Ethan's wife, Emily, is talking to Chelsea, Ethan and Reed's sister, and her boyfriend, Mayson. Ethan and Mayson were in the military together, and a couple of months ago, he showed up with a gunshot wound and fighting for his life. This family's close bond is what everyone wishes for.

"One of these days," Ethan says, "we are going to get here before everyone and be the first in line." We all laugh, and Emily just shakes her head, knowing full well we'll never be first in line. There are just too many people in line, and usually, we let the older generation eat first.

"One can hope," Emily says. I listen half-heartedly as I feel Amelia get in line next to me.

She pushes my shoulder, and I look at her sideways. I'm about to tell her she's a pain in my ass when all of our phones go off. I take my phone out and see the code for fire from the alarm company.

I look up into the sky and see the black smoke off in the distance. "One of the barns is on fire!" I don't know who says it, but I'm running to my truck when I hear it.

Ethan is right beside me as we jump into my truck. I never park in the driveway, opting to park in the road so I can just leave. "Fuck, fuck, fuck," he says as I pull out, the sound of the tires screeching behind me. My heart beats so fast in my chest all I can do is hear the echo. My stomach sinks as I get closer and closer, yet the smoke that fills the sky makes me feel farther and farther away.

"Which barn?" I ask and then look over when he doesn't answer.

"Your house," he says, and I swallow the lump in my throat. I look at the road as I try to remember if I turned off the coffee maker this morning. I unplugged it as soon as I was done. My head spins as I try to retrace my every step that I took today.

"I double-check everything when I leave," I say. When I came to town six months ago, I bumped into Ethan at the diner. He said his family farm was always hiring and told me to swing by the day after. I was staying at the town motel and was about to head back out of town when I got the job. At first, it was just as a ranch hand, doing odd jobs here and there. Nothing big at the time. But they liked how I worked, so they gave me a company truck and asked me to take over as ranch supervisor, putting me in charge of making sure the ranch had everything they needed to operate. Ethan and Casey both trained me, and it didn't hurt that it came with an apartment in one of the barns.

"Firemen are four minutes out," Ethan says, and my eyes follow the black smoke in the sky. Instead of getting closer and closer to me, they are getting thicker and thicker in the sky.

"We just had the hay delivered," I say. "It's stocked up full." I try to calm my heart as I make my way to the barn. Every single second feels like an hour.

When I turn off the road onto the gravel driveway, I hear the rocks hitting the truck with how fast I'm going. I look behind me and see the dust coming up, but I also see five trucks following us and hear the sound of the sirens off in the distance.

"Maybe we can contain it," I say. Only when we get closer, the sight of the thick smoke makes my stomach sink. My eyes find the barn, and I don't need anyone to tell me that there is no way anything can be salvaged. I stop the truck on the side and get out, not bothering to close my door. I look over and see the red fire truck racing down the driveway. It stops, and the eight firemen jump out of their truck while another truck stops beside them.

It feels like I'm in a movie, and this isn't real. The heat from the fire sinks into my skin, and the closer and closer we get, the more my eyes feel the burn.

The red barn is engulfed in flames. The orange and yellow flames come out of the top two windows that were my bedroom. The sound of crackling fills the quiet air as all the men at the barbecue stand to the side, watching the barn go up in flames.

The sound of shattering glass fills the air. Two firemen

stand on top of the fire truck, their hoses spraying water toward the roof. Six other firemen beside the blaze try to contain it. The heat from the fire hits my skin, but nothing could make me move from this spot.

I watch in shock from the sidelines with everyone else as the firemen do their best to contain it. I hear yelling going on around them, but I can't move. I hear car doors slamming, and I know more people are arriving, but I can't look away.

My eyes fixate on the flames coming out of the window, the doors, and the sides of the walls. Yellow, orange, and red mix, making everything in front of me look hazy. *How can this be happening?* How the fuck am I going to recover from this? I put my hands on my head now as my eyes sting from the flames.

The sound of crackling starts, and all I can do is watch in horror as the roof suddenly vanishes. My hand flies to my mouth as everything I own goes up in flames.

Two

Amelia

I LOOK UP into the sky and see the black smoke. "Oh my God." I put my hand to my mouth for a minute, turning around in a circle. Or maybe it's the earth spinning.

The sound of yelling snaps me out of my daydream or nightmare, making me look toward the driveway. The men run to their trucks, the sound of rocks hitting metal as one truck peels out.

"I want someone at each barn." My grandfather walks past me, talking to one of the ranch hands. "I want someone making sure all the horses are okay," he says.

"Grandpa," I call for him, and he turns around, the worry clear on his face.

"We can take the horses," I say, and he shakes his head.

"Don't you put any ideas in any of your heads. You do not leave this farm." He points at me, his voice stern like it was when we were younger, and he knew we were going to get into trouble. "And I mean it, Amelia." He turns to walk away.

I wait until he's far enough away before I turn around and look at Chelsea. If anyone is going to come with me, it would have to be Chelsea. We've been stuck at the hip growing up, and if there was trouble, we found it.

"Let's go," Chelsea says, huffing out, and Willow and Emily both look at her. "You know that us staying here is going to be hell." She looks back at me, and I just nod. "So I'm going. Who is coming with me?"

"Me," I say without missing a beat, and then look back at Emily, who nods at us.

"I have to make sure the kids are alright," Emily says, walking over to my mother and handing her my niece.

My mother looks at my niece and then looks up at me. She shakes her head but then mouths to me, "Be careful."

I nod my head and look back at Willow, who is tapping her index finger on her pants. "He's not going to like this," she says of Quinn. "He especially said don't move from here." She looks up at the smoke filling the sky, and this time, it looks thicker than it did before.

I look over at the barn and see them starting to bring out the horses. They take off in every single direction. Some with two riders and some with three but none alone. I see my grandfather race off also.

I turn back to see people packing up the food. Knowing

my grandmother, she'll make dinners for everyone and have someone run it over to the men.

Emily runs back to us as we look up again and see the smoke getting thicker and thicker. "Let's go," I say, and we run to Chelsea's car.

I get into the front seat and look back to see the tears rolling down Willow's face. "Is it the barn?" She wipes away the tears, and Emily reaches over and hugs her. "The horses." Willow has been in town for a couple of months, and she's had a rough start after being left for dead. She started working at one of the rehab barns that Quinn owns and is very close to one of the horses.

"Hope is fine," I say, and the look of relief falls all over her. "It's the supply barn." I take one more look at Emily and then turn to look out the window.

"Wait, isn't that …?" she says, and I just nod my head and don't say the words everyone is thinking. Our childhood barn. The barn we grew up at. The barn where all the kids took their first riding lesson. That barn was our second home. If we were having a bad day, chances are we would be at the barn, and within an hour, it would be okay. I wipe the tear from the corner of my eye as I send up a silent prayer that everyone is safe.

None of us says anything while we travel toward the barn. Chelsea drives faster than she should to get us there. I look toward the blue sky and hope that the black smoke will stop, but it doesn't stop. "What are the chances?" I say and look over at Chelsea. "That."

"Whatever it is," Chelsea says softly. "As long as no one is hurt, we can rebuild." Everyone is stuck in their own thoughts, so I focus on the black smoke in the sky.

We see the trucks all parked along the road, so Chelsea pulls over to the side of the road. We get out of the truck and hear the men yelling through the trees. We walk down the driveway filled with cars. We start feeling the heat, but we can't see the barn yet with the trees surrounding us. But as soon as we get close enough, we see the barn, and all four of us halt with a gasp. My feet stick like glue to the grass as I look on in horror.

The red barn is engulfed in flames. The two windows on the top floor are busted out, and orange and yellow flames escape from the holes. The red paint looks like it's melting off the wood. A fire truck is on each side of the barn with the stainless-steel ladders extended, and two firemen aim their hoses at the top of the roof to douse the flames. I see other firemen on the side at a safe distance as they extinguish the flames lower down. I hear yelling all around them as they work overtime to save what they can.

We make our way over to where the men stand. Willow goes to stand beside Quinn, her hand going into his. You can see the tears in his eyes as he pulls her close to him. Chelsea walks to Mayson, and he puts an arm around her shoulder, pulling her to him. Ethan looks around and spots Emily right away, shaking his head but holding out his hand. I walk to stand beside Asher, who stands beside my father. My father looks over, and we share a look as we both look back at the barn.

The sound of yelling echoes as I feel like I'm watching the scene from out of my body. My eyes fixate on the red and yellow of the flames.

The crackling sound is so loud it makes me come out of my daze. And it all happens in slow motion as we hear more crackling sounds. I look at the firemen yelling something, and then watch as the top of the roof falls to one side, and then the middle collapses in front of our eyes. The heat of the fire rushes to us, and we have to put our hands up to shield our faces.

"Oh my God." I hear from beside me and look back at Asher, who watches the barn go up in flames.

I put my hand on his arm, but his eyes just stare straight ahead. Nothing I can say to him right now will make things better. My hand falls from his arm as I stare ahead at the barn, where I had my first kiss.

The orange flames work their way through the four walls. One of the firemen comes over to us, walking straight up to my father. "You need to step back." He puts his hand on his helmet as he listens to the scramble from his walkie-talkie. "The whole thing is going to go." He looks over at my father. "Jacob, we need you to secure the perimeter. No one in or out."

"Already on it. My guys have been called and have started closing down the roads," my father says, turning to look at us. "Guys, I need you to move away."

He comes to stand in front of me, and I don't notice the tears running down my face. "It's going to be okay, honey," he says and wraps his arms around me. "Everyone is safe."

"I know," I say in a whisper, and I move out of his arms because I know he has work to do.

"You going to be okay?" he asks, and I nod. He doesn't have time to make sure I'm okay. "Ethan," he calls out to my brother. "I'm going to need help."

Ethan kisses Emily's head and walks toward my dad. "We need to get some tape up all around."

"I can help," Asher says from beside me, and we both look at him.

"Asher," my father says softly. "Are you sure?" He looks over at the barn. "You just lost …"

"Yeah," he says, putting his hands on his hips and letting out a deep breath. "I just lost everything. Not the first time either." He looks over to the barn, his eyes squinting. "With my luck, it probably won't be the last." He bends his head and walks away toward my father's truck, where Ethan is grabbing the yellow tape.

"I can't even imagine," I say softly and look over at my father. "What can I do to help?"

"Honestly," my father says, looking around. "The only thing we can do is stay out of the way."

He bends to kiss my cheek before walking away.

I watch as he walks over to the men hovering around his truck. I see my father pointing in different directions and giving orders. My eyes fall on Asher, his shoulders slumped as he listens to my father. I want to rush over to him and tell him it's going to be okay. I want to hug him and tell him I'm here for him. When he came onto the scene six months ago, I thought he was the sexiest man I'd ever seen. Then we started working side by side, and I found out that he had the best intentions. He would give you the shirt off his back if it would help you. Every single day, I lusted after him more and more, but I knew it would go nowhere. It didn't stop us from flirting with each other, but in the end, neither of us would be willing to take that step.

The sound of cracking has everyone looking back over to see one side of the barn start to teeter and then slowly crumble to the ground. The heat comes toward us right away, and I put my hand toward my face. It happens in slow motion, and I don't even know I'm holding my breath. The remaining walls sway side to side as if they're balancing on the edge, and in a blink of an eye, the rest of the barn comes crashing down.

I put my hand in front of my mouth to muffle my scream. I feel heat beside me and look to see Chelsea there, her arm going around my shoulder. "It's gone," I say, wiping away a tear rolling down my cheek. No matter how many I wipe away, there are more to follow. "It's all gone."

"We'll get it back," she says softly, and then I feel someone put their hand in mine and look over to see Willow.

Her own tears are on her face. "It's going to be okay," she says. "It's going to be okay."

I just nod my head as we watch the firemen work at putting out the fire. "We should go," Emily says. "Get out of the way."

I nod and then turn to walk away. I take a couple of steps, then turn back to take one more look at it. With the back of my palm, I wipe away the tears that continue to fall, no matter how many times I wipe them away. "It'll be okay," Willow says from beside me.

We walk like snails back to the car, all of us looking down and lost in our own thoughts. We see police tape at the front of the lane, and when I look to the side, I see Asher and Ethan wrapping the same tape around a couple of trees. Willow and Emily get into the back seat of the car as I pull open my door, but I stop, looking across the street. Though there are rows and rows of blooming trees, all I can see is black smoke, but for some reason, I feel eyes on me.

"What is it?" Chelsea gets back out of the car and looks at me, her eyes turning to see what I'm looking at.

"Nothing," I say, shaking my head and getting in the car. I close the door and fasten my seat belt. "I guess I'm just feeling out of it," I say, and my eyes try to look into the dark forest, but all I can see is darkness.

SOUTHERN SECRETS SOUTHERN

Three

Asher

I WALK TOWARD Jacob's truck with my head down. I don't even think about what I've lost, not when I looked over and saw Amelia with tears running down her cheeks. It made my stomach sink and burn. I wanted to go and comfort her, take her in my arms and tell her how sorry I was. The guilt that this accident could have been my fault rushed through me. We both looked at the blaze as the firemen tried their best to put it out as fast as possible, everyone working together.

"Asher," Jacob calls my name softly, and I look up at him. "If you want to sit this one out …"

I shake my head. "Sitting around and dwelling on this isn't going to do anybody any good," I say.

"We'll replace everything," Ethan says, putting his

hand on my shoulder and squeezing. "Or we'll try to anyway."

"You don't have to do that," I say. "I never had much to begin with." I shake my head, looking back at the barn. "Besides, you guys lost more than I did." I look at him, and he just looks back at the place where the barn used to stand. The orange flames burn through what remains on the ground.

As far back as I can remember, everything I've ever owned has fit in one plastic bag. It was a white grocery store bag with two handles. Until this fire, I still had the bag with me. I could never just throw it away. Instead, I tucked it under the clothes I had.

I was placed into foster care when I was four years old. My mother dropped me off at the babysitter with a kiss on my head, telling me she would see me later.

"There is nothing else I can do," the babysitter hissed at her husband, who was sitting beside me on the worn brown and yellow couch. She picked up the phone again. "This isn't funny. If you don't call me back in the next thirty minutes, I have no choice but to call the cops."

I looked from the babysitter back to the television, my stomach rumbling from not eating since I had been there. "Would you feed the kid?" her husband barked when my stomach kept interrupting what the guy on the television was saying.

With a huff, she grabbed me by my arm and brought me back into the kitchen. She set me at the table and said, "Your mother will be here soon." I just nodded and looked over at her. I waited and waited while she made mac and cheese, and for a four-year-old, it felt like forever, but she finally placed it in front of me.

Hearing a knock on the door made me look up, and I suddenly remembered how happy I was, knowing that my mom was there. I ran to the front door, only to be confronted by two police officers. They came in the front door and then went into the kitchen while I was told to sit on the couch. I couldn't really hear anything but their mumbling. Another knock on the door made me get up, thinking for sure this was my mother.

The door opened, and a woman came in, dressed in a long skirt and a white shirt. I remember looking at her and wondering if my mom sent her to come get me. Her friends were always picking me up and taking me places.

The woman went to the kitchen, giving me a sad smile on the way there, and I just didn't understand what was going on. "Looks like you are going into the system," the husband said from beside me. "It was just a matter of time."

One of the police officers came back out with the woman who just got there. "Hi, Asher," the woman said, sitting down next to me. "I'm Shauna, and this is Detective Moro." She pointed at the police officer standing in his blue uniform. "We are going to take you somewhere while we find your mom."

I wanted to laugh at the irony of it. I slept at someone's house that night. I woke up the next day, hoping that my mom would be there, but for the next three days, it was the same story. No one knew anything. No one paid attention to me. The person fed me two meals a day and made sure that when Shauna came to see me, I was clean. For three days, I tried to stay awake. I constantly looked out the window for my mom, convinced she would come soon. But that wasn't how the story would end. Four days later, they found her lying on a stainless-steel stretcher in the morgue.

She was in the car with a guy driving high and drunk and ran head-on into the median on the highway. I was a ward of the state from that day on, jumping from one foster home to the next. It didn't take me long to realize I was a paycheck for all of them, and trust me, they let me know each day.

I feel someone push me to the side, and I blink away the memories. There is no time to dwell on the past. That was my motto from when I turned thirteen. Turning my head, I see all the men have gathered around us. Ethan stands beside me, and Beau is next to him. Casey comes close to us, but he stands just outside of the circle. His hands are going crazy on his phone. My eyes go back to the ground as I listen to Jacob give orders.

"Gentlemen," he starts. "The fire marshal wants us to secure the premises," Jacob says, and I look at him, the pounding in my head intensifying. "The fire marshal just said he doesn't think this fire will be out anytime soon." He looks at me, then at the other guys. "It's going to be a long night." He stops talking when he looks up and sees Casey coming back to us.

All eyes turn to him when he stands beside Jacob. "Just got off the phone with my father. He said there has been no activity on the other farms." He looks down.

"But until we get any report from the fire chief, I want us to keep our eyes open." He looks at us, and I nod at him.

"Okay, let's get this closed off and see what else we can do," Jacob says and turns to hand Ethan a roll of tape.

"I'll go with Ethan," I say, and Jacob looks up at me and nods.

"We are going to close off the right side of the driveway," Ethan tells his father as he points in that direction. I hear Beau and Mayson talk about taking the other side, but I just put my head down and walk away with Ethan.

The heat hits my back right away. "We'll get it all back," Ethan says, and I look over at him, then back down at the green grass. "Whatever you lost in there, my family will make sure that you get it all back."

I stop walking and turn to look back, thinking that maybe it looks worse than it is, but then one side of the barn falls, and the dust and black smoke fill the air. "Whatever I had in there wasn't anything that I can't replace." He holds out the tape for me. "Let's just make sure no one gets hurt." It's Ethan's turn to nod. I walk toward a tree while he holds the tape, my eyes going to the barn as I see the flames still going. I wrap the yellow caution tape around the tree, then make my way over to one of the gate posts. The heat from the fire hits me right away.

We secure the one spot, making sure anyone coming by can see the tape and not enter.

The air smells of burned wood. Anyone who didn't

know would think we were having a bonfire. With the help of all the guys, we secure and make sure all entries to the barn are blocked off. The sweat drips from me as we get closer and closer to the burning barn, trying to close off as close as we can to make sure everyone stays safe.

The sound of the firemen yelling makes us look back over at the barn. We see the firemen running away from the barn, and the sound of crackling fills the silence as the rest of the barn falls to the ground. The rush of heat we feel has us holding up our arms to block our face.

We stand here in stunned silence. In a matter of hours, what is left is a pile of debris with the flames still going.

The sun goes down, and the only things that light up the barn are the lights from the two fire trucks. Jacob has us all bring our vehicles to the barn and shine our headlights in order to help.

"There is food over there. You guys should eat something," Jacob says, coming to Ethan and me with two water bottles in his hands.

"Thank you." I open the bottle and gulp down the cold water.

"The fire chief came to talk to me," Jacob says, his voice going lower so he's not overheard.

I stop drinking when I see him look at me, and then his eyes go down. Something about his look makes the water I just drank work its way back up. "What is it?" The fear that this fire was my fault has been playing in my head over and over again. How the fuck was I going to pay to replace the whole barn? How the fuck would I be able to look into anyone's eyes, knowing I destroyed their barn? How the fuck would I be able to forgive myself? The shock and numbness take over now, and I feel hollow inside.

"He can't confirm it for sure," Jacob says, my head falling as I wait for him to accuse me. But instead, the words that come out of his mouth shock me even more. "But he did say that it looks like arson."

Four

AMELIA

LOOKING OUT THE window, I see the black smoke starting to thin out. "You okay?" I hear from beside me and look over at Chelsea.

"Not really," I say honestly as she pushes me over with her hip to wash her hands. We've been at my grandmother's house ever since we walked away from the fire. "How are you doing?" I ask, and she looks down at her hands.

"I thought cooking and baking would make me feel better." She turns the water off and grabs a dish cloth to dry her hands. She looks out the same window I was just looking out. "It's not."

"Has anyone texted you?" I ask, and she grabs the phone from her pocket as she checks it. "No, nothing." I look around the kitchen at my grandmother, who hasn't stopped cooking since this happened even though my mother and aunt have been trying to force her to sit down.

I look back outside. "I need some air," I say, and she takes a step to follow me. "Go sit down. You haven't eaten anything today."

She glares at me. "I can sit outside," she says, and I'm about to argue with her when my grandmother calls her over.

I take the opportunity while she's busy to slip outside. The sun is slowly setting, and the smell of fire is still in the air. I sit down on the top step and look up at the gray sky. My eyes fixate on the smoke, and I don't hear the footsteps until someone sits beside me.

"Hey, sweetheart." I look over to see my grandfather put his arms around my shoulders and pull me to him, kissing my temple. He lets out a big deep breath. "What are you doing outside?"

"Is the fire under control?" I ask. His whole face looks tired and his eyes worried.

"Last I heard," he says. "Just about."

I put my head on his shoulder just like I used to do when I was a little girl. Heck, I still do it. "Don't worry, Grandpa. We'll build it back even better."

He chuckles a little. "Oh, if I know my kids, it'll be brand new in a week with all these new gadgets."

It's my turn to laugh. My grandparents have lived on this farm their whole life and my great-grandparents before them. Then my uncle Casey came in and brought in technology. Let's just say my grandfather is not too pleased with it. "I set off the sprinklers last time I opened his iPad."

"I'll teach you, Grandpa." I kiss his cheek. "Let me go and get you something to eat."

I start to get up, and he gets up with me. "If I don't tell your grandmother I'm here, I'll never hear the end of it."

We walk into the house together, and my grandmother comes over and gives him a hug. He doesn't stay to eat. Instead, he grabs some food to take to the men.

I kiss everyone goodbye at midnight and make my way home. I don't bother catching a ride. Instead, I walk in the field. The same field I grew up in. I bet if you blindfolded us all, we would still know how to get to our houses.

The warm breeze blows softly as I walk up the back steps of my house. My little, small house that I bought without my parents knowing.

I press the keypad, and the door clicks open. I make my way to the couch and sit down for a second. Laying my head back, I close my eyes for just a minute. Or so I thought.

The soft alarm makes my eyes spring open as I jump off the couch and grab my phone from the coffee table. I turn the alarm off and scroll to see if anyone has texted me.

The last text I got was from Chelsea at three.

Chelsea: Mayson just got home. Fire is finally out.

I don't bother answering her in case she's sleeping. Instead, I close my eyes for just a couple of seconds before I roll off the couch and walk toward my bedroom.

My whole body feels like it was run over by a semi. I pull my shirt over my head and throw it in the dirty laundry before starting the shower.

Slipping off my jeans, I get into the shower and put my head back. I still smell of smoke, and I was only there for a short time. I close my eyes, and all I can see is the barn again. All I can see is the fire. I can't believe that this nightmare is my reality. I put my hands on my face as I sob into them silently.

Getting out, I dress in another pair of jeans and a T-shirt, then slide on my worn boots. I walk out of the house and see that the sun is slowly coming up. It takes me two minutes to get to the barn, and when I get there, I'm surprised to see the lights on.

The smell of coffee hits me as soon as I walk into the barn, and I almost groan. "Good morning," I say to no one in particular. I hear the sound of hay moving when I see Willow stick her head out of her horse's stall.

"Good morning," she says, looking just like I feel. "You're here early."

I look over at the clock and see that it's not even past five. "Couldn't sleep," I say. "Figured I'd get here and bang out the paperwork in case I need to help with deliveries." I walk to my office and open the door. I toss my keys on the desk and turn around to go to the coffee machine.

I walk out and spot Quinn. "Hey," I say, surprised to see him. "What are you doing here?"

He chuckles, and then I hear Willow from behind him walking to us. "That is what I asked him, too," she says.

I grab my coffee mug off the shelf and fill it to the rim.

"Well, for one …" Quinn says. I turn to look back at him, bringing the hot coffee to my lips. "I own this." He puts his hands on his hips. You can tell from his eyes that he hasn't slept yet.

When we were growing up, he always had this need to help and nurture, so it was no surprise when he decided to open his own equine therapy farm. I thought he would do well. What I wasn't expecting was for him to open seven of them. When he opened the first one, he asked me to help him with the paperwork. It was supposed to be for a month until he got up and running. Once that month was over, he asked me to stay on for a couple of months. Needless to say, five years later, I'm still here, and I love every minute of it.

"Okay, so you own this place. It doesn't mean you can't take a day off," Willow says from beside him. "You didn't even sleep." She looks up at him.

"I'll sleep tonight," he tells her and kisses her lips. "There is work to do, and I'll just go crazy sitting at home."

"How bad is it?" I ask. When I left my grandmother's house at midnight, they were still out there.

"The fire is out," he says, huffing out. "But the barn is ashes. There is nothing left of it."

"That is crazy," I say, shaking my head and taking another long gulp of coffee and feeling the burn all the way down. My mind spins now, and I want to ask about Asher, but the last thing I want anyone to think is that I have a thing for him. We work together, and even though we flirt, we always do it when no one is around.

"Whatever it is, we are going to make it better," Quinn says. "From now on, we have two other barns that are going to be the headquarters." I nod and look at him.

"I'm assuming Asher is taking the day off," I say. He just looks at me, and we hear the gravel outside crunch.

"I'm going to take that as a no." Willow shakes her head and turns to walk back into her horse's stall. My eyes go to the barn door, and I watch Asher walk in.

He walks with his head down, not expecting us to be here. He stops walking when he feels eyes on him. "Hey," he says softly. "I didn't know anyone would be here so early." He's wearing the same clothes as yesterday, and you can smell the smoke on him. I swallow down the lump starting to grow in my throat as I think of him alone all night long with no one to hold his hand.

"What are you doing here?" Quinn says, and Asher shrugs. "Did you even sleep?"

"Nah," he says, coming to the coffee machine. I move aside so he can get his coffee. "Need a refill?" he asks me softly with the coffee pot still in his hand. I shake my head, and he puts the pot back and takes a deep gulp of coffee. I look over at him as he leans back on the counter next to me. I would normally go to my office now, but the need to stay beside him is strong.

"I thought I heard my father tell you that if you came in today, you would be fired," Quinn says, and I laugh and roll my eyes. My uncle Casey has fired me at least once a week for working longer than I should.

"Well, I'll make sure to stay clear of him," Asher says,

and I throw my head back and laugh.

"You know he gets live videos from the farms, right?" Quinn tells him, and Asher just looks at him, not at all bothered by this news. "You haven't even taken a shower," Quinn points out to him.

"I can attest to that," I say, and Asher looks over at me and glares. His brown eyes look almost black. The redness of his eyes is also very apparent. "You stink."

"I have a bag of clothes," Quinn says, "that Willow packed for you. It's in the office. Go to my house and take a shower."

"I'm not going to your house," Asher says, shaking his head. "I'm not going to intrude like that."

"Then take my keys," I say the words before I can stop them. "You can stay with me. I live alone and have two spare bedrooms." *Fuck, fuck, fuck,* my head thinks when I hear the words that have just come out of them. It's one thing to be friendly and everything at work, but it's another thing to have him under my roof. I mean, it's not like I'm home often. Between here and the bar, I only go home to sleep.

"Um," Asher says.

I know I should just take it as a no and walk to my office and shut my mouth. My brain knows this but my mouth, not so much. "I won't take no for an answer, and if you push me, I'll call my grandfather." I smirk. "Casey you can say no to, but you have never ever said no to my grandfather." *Just shut up already*, I groan inwardly. I'm ready to duct-tape my own mouth to stop shit from coming out of it.

"I don't need to stay with you," Asher says. "I can get a room at the motel."

"Then I'll tell my grandmother," I counter. "Not sure which one you want me to tell." *If I don't do this, I'll feel guilty about him staying alone*, I tell myself.

"You're a bully," he says, and I shrug.

"I've been called worse," I joke. "Last week, you called me a raging lunatic."

"You told me that you hoped bees ate my junk." He shakes his head. He lets go of a deep breath, and I want to rub his back, but instead, I clutch my mug tighter. "But I really need a shower."

"Keys are on my desk. Why don't you sleep for a bit and then come in at noon?" I suggest, and he looks at the clock and then back at Quinn.

"Or come back tomorrow," Quinn says. "Tomorrow will be good."

"Are you going to ride my ass all day if I don't leave?" He looks at me.

I tilt my head to the side and smirk. "I don't know what you mean by that," I say innocently, "but if you mean, will I tell every single family member who calls me today that you are here and haven't showered or slept?" I stop at the entrance of my office. "The answer to that would be a big fat yes."

He groans, and I walk to my desk to grab the keys I just tossed there. I stop and pick up the black bag that Willow put there and bring it out to him. "Here." I walk to him and hand him the keys and the bag.

"Fine," he says, huffing out. "I'll see you later." He

puts his mug in the sink and then walks out.

I watch him walk out of the barn and then feel eyes on me. "Are we going to talk about this?" Quinn says, and I just stare at him.

"Nothing to talk about. The man is homeless," I say, ignoring the thumping of my heart against my chest. "What would you expect me to do?"

"We could have set him up at an empty house," Quinn says, and I fold my arms over my chest and roll my eyes, shaking my head.

"You think that man"—I point at the door Asher just walked out of—"would have taken you up on an offer to stay in a house that has been sitting empty for the past six months?" I don't give him a chance to answer me. "Tell me, did you not offer him that house instead of sleeping in a barn?" Quinn just glares at me. "I thought so."

"Whatever," Quinn says, turning and walking away. "I'm telling your father you are living with a boy."

I watch his retreating back. "Snitches get stitches!"

Five

Asher

I GET BACK into the truck, and even with the windows open, I smell the smoke. I knew I should have just gone to a motel after I left the barn at three a.m., but instead, I sat on the hood of the truck and watched the empty space where the barn used to sit.

My head spun with regret the whole time. The dark sky was slowly turning a soft pink when I finally got off the truck while my head screamed at me that I needed to stop dwelling and get over it. I walked into the barn, making a mental list of the things I had to do. I wasn't expecting Quinn to be there or to see Amelia standing there with him. I should have taken Quinn up on his offer to use his place, but I didn't know how Willow would feel. She just started getting comfortable around me, and

I didn't want to ruin that.

I pull up to Amelia's house and turn off the truck. Her house is a perfect size, and I've even thought about buying one like hers. I just didn't know if I wanted to call this place home. Grabbing the black bag, I get out of the truck, looking toward the front of the house.

I walk up the path past the garden in the front with perfect flowers. I know that this is all Amelia. Unlike her other cousins who love to cook, she is a more *get your hands dirty to relax* kind of person. Three steps lead me to the blue door, and when I unlock it, the cold air escapes like I just opened the freezer.

I kick off my boots at the front door and place the keys on the hook right beside the light switch. I take a second to look around. I have been in here a total of two times. Both times were with Quinn—one was to move her bed and the other was to help hook up her television on the brick wall to my left.

I walk past the living room and the L- shaped couch facing the brick wall with the television. The living room spills into the dining room, and I know the spare bedrooms are on the right side, and her bedroom is on the left. I feel like I'm intruding on her privacy by being here by myself. I look at the pictures on the wall when I turn toward the spare bedroom. There are three pictures on the wall, one on top of the other.

The top one is a picture of Amelia with her grandfather, her smile huge as she hugs him. I don't care what he says; she's his favorite. The middle one is of her with Quinn and Chelsea. The three of them are laughing at something only they understand or some inside joke. Then the last one is of her and Chelsea with her head thrown back laughing. The candid shots look like they were taken not too long ago.

I walk toward the first bedroom and stop in my tracks. This has to be the nicest spare bedroom I've seen in my life. Usually, a spare bedroom is just a bed, but not here. A king-size bed fills the room with a cast-iron bed frame. The white cover on the bed looks too nice to even touch. A checkered black-and-white cover is folded at the end of the bed with matching pillows.

Turning, I walk to the next room, which is the bathroom. After dumping the bag on the floor, I push the shower curtain to the side and turn on the water. I strip out of the smoke-soaked clothes and toss them in a pile on the floor.

I step under the hot water and close my eyes, stopping the burning for just a minute. I put my hands on the white tiles on the wall, and when I open my hands, I see that the black is coming off it. The water is turning gray at my feet. I hang my head down, letting the hot water seep into my skin. I spend more time in the shower than I ever have, washing twice to make sure I get the smoke off my skin. When I step out, I grab a white towel and wipe my face to see if anything black comes off.

Opening the black bag, I grab the shorts and slip them on. Walking out of the bathroom, I go back to the bedroom. I think about slipping under the covers, but instead, I walk out and go lie on the couch. It takes me less than thirty seconds to fall asleep.

I hear walking, and my eyes open slowly, and it takes me a minute to figure out where I'm at. Looking to the left, I see the brick wall, and then I hear movement coming from the kitchen. The house is darker, and I look to see that someone has closed the drapes. I sit up and look at Amelia in the kitchen, trying to be as quiet as she can. "Hey," I say, my voice groggy as I get up.

"I'm so sorry. I tried to be quiet," she says. I see that she's tied her hair up on top of her head, and she's wearing shorts. "Why are you on the couch?" she asks, reaching into the cupboard to pull out another plate.

I walk past her wooden dining table with two long benches and a vase of fresh roses in the middle. "The bed looked too clean to sleep on," I say and run my hand through my hair.

She stops moving and just looks at me. "What bed?"

I look at her and point toward the bedroom. "The one with the white bedspread and the black-and-white-checkered blanket."

She puts her head back and laughs. "Chelsea threw up on that bed two weeks ago."

"Gross," I say, shaking my head. "Can I get a glass of water?"

"Help yourself," she says. "Cups are there"—she points at a door—"and drinks are in there"—she points at the fridge. "You can also help yourself to some chicken pot pie."

"You cooked?" I ask, going over to the cupboard and pulling it open to grab a glass. I look over at her as she grabs her plate and goes toward the dining room table. I walk over to the stainless-steel fridge and grab the water she has in the glass container. I look around her white kitchen with a big white and gray island. The rustic brown cupboards under the island make it seem like a farmhouse.

"My grandmother has enough food to feed the whole state," she says, sitting down with her back toward me.

I look over and see that it's just past two. "I slept six hours straight."

"Lucky," she says as she chews. "I got four hours."

"When did you get home?" I ask, grabbing a serving of pie and walking over to the dining room table.

"Quinn kicked me out at eight," she says while I sit down in front of her.

"Quinn?" I ask, surprised.

"My grandmother and grandfather came," she says, and I laugh. "They threatened us all." She rolls her eyes. "Willow got scared that they would 'die.'" She uses air quotes. I look at her confused. "According to them, they worry about us so much they could die."

I shake my head. "Thank you," I say while I eat, "for feeling sorry for me."

"Oh, I didn't feel sorry for you. I felt sorry for anyone who had to smell you." She scrunches her nose as she finishes eating. She gets up. "I'm going to go and see if I can get another couple of hours before I go to the bar."

I try not to watch her walk toward the kitchen, but my eyes deceive me, the shorts tight enough to mold to her ass. My cock springs to action, and when she turns around, my eyes fly to my plate as my heart speeds up at being caught by her. It's not the first time my cock has sprung for her. It's literally an everyday occurrence at this point, and no matter how many times I tell myself to get over her, my body fights with me.

"I'll let myself out," I say, raising my head.

"Take your time," she says, walking back to her bedroom and closing the door behind her. I finish my plate and clean up before I walk back to the bedroom and look in the bag. I grab the boxers and then slip on the jeans next with a T-shirt that fits me just a touch too tight. I turn and see that the jeans are tight on my ass. I squat down, hoping to stretch them, but nothing happens.

I grab the bag and stuff my old clothes in my hand. I slip on my boots and softly close the door behind me.

I take my phone out and see that I have a couple of texts checking up on me and another couple of phone calls from Billy and Charlotte. Never in my life have I had someone worry about if I was okay, but this family has taken me in with open arms. Not once have they looked down on me. When I first came into town, I had five dollars left. I was one day away from eating from the dumpster when Ethan not only gave me a job but also gave me shelter.

I toss the bag on the seat and throw the clothes in the garbage can. I get into the truck and make my way back over to the barn. The sun's shining high, and the heat hits my arms right away.

Parking the truck on the side of the road, I spot Jacob's sheriff truck at the entrance. I make my way toward the barn, ducking under the yellow tape. Even though I knew there was no barn there, seeing it again in the sunlight makes me stop in my tracks. Knowing that it's gone and seeing it with my own eyes knocks me on my ass. The lump in my throat grows when I see that everything is dust. Jacob and Ethan both walk around, looking down at the ground around the barn.

Ethan must sense someone is here because he looks up and starts laughing. "What the fuck are you wearing?" he asks, making Jacob look in my direction.

"I borrowed clothes from Quinn," I tell them, walking toward them.

Jacob laughs when I finally stand in front of him. "If you lather yourself in oil, you might pass for one of those calendar boys." I shake my head.

"I'm going to buy clothes after this," I tell them, looking around.

"I can't believe nothing is left." I walk, stepping on some of the debris, picking up a piece of tin. "When do we start cleanup?"

"We are trying to see if anything here is out of place," Jacob says.

"What are you looking for exactly?" I ask. Getting up, I look around, walking through the ashes.

"Anything you think shouldn't be here," Ethan says, and I watch as they make their way down different sides. Something white catches my eyes in the grass a couple of feet from where the side of the barn used to be.

Once I get there, I squat down and pick up the white piece and hold it in my hand. "Jacob," I call his name, and they both look at me. "Would a cigarette be out of place?"

Six

AMELIA

THE ALARM WAKES me up, and I reach out of my blanket to turn it off, then bring my arm back under the thick heavy white duvet cover. I turn onto my back and stretch, my body hurting from staying up most of the night.

I toss the cover off me and get out of bed. If I stayed in bed any longer, I would not get up. Walking into my bathroom, I go straight to my walk-in closet and grab the black jeans and a black tank top. Dressing, I walk to the bathroom and look at my reflection. My eyes look like I haven't slept in weeks. Turning on the cold water, I fill my hands and then splash it on my face. Reaching for a towel, I dab my face and grab some makeup to make me look human.

Slipping on my cowboy boots, I grab a jean jacket and walk out the door. My phone rings as soon as I sit in the car, and I see it's my mother.

"Hey, Momma," I say as I connect my phone to the Bluetooth.

"Hey, baby girl," she says, and I smile every single time she calls me that. I could be fifty, and she would still call me baby girl. "Where are you?"

"I'm in the car on the way to the bar." I pull out of my driveway.

"Did you even sleep?" she asks, and I chuckle. "Don't you laugh at me, Amelia Charlotte McIntyre."

"Ohhh, full name always means business," I say softly. "I'm fine, Mom."

"You are burning the candle at both ends, baby girl," she says softly. "And you know what happens then."

"We get another candle," I joke with her.

When the bar comes into view, my face lights up in a smile. This is what I'm working myself to the bone for. The bar is owned by my aunt Savannah. When we were little, we used to be able to come here on special occasions when she would have family day. I had the most fun line dancing with Chelsea and my aunts to playing hide-and-seek behind the bar. When I turned eighteen, I begged her to give me a summer job. She was adamant about me only working during the day when she was there. It took me a week to beg her to give me a Saturday night. She only agreed because she was stuck, and she was working. It was the most fun I've had in my life behind the bar mixing drinks and laughing with everyone. I knew then and there that this is what I wanted to do. I wanted to own the bar. I worked part-time even when I was in college, and finally, when I got my business degree, I went to see her. I sat down with her and asked her what it would take for me to buy the bar from her.

She was shocked that was what I wanted to do, and with tears in her eyes, she took out the papers to the bar and was ready to sign it over to me for fifty cents. I refused it; I would not just take it from her. I want to own it outright. I want it to be mine. We agreed on a price, and every single month, I pay her until it is paid off. It was supposed to take me ten years, but I've done it in less than five, and I only have four more payments to go.

"I really wish you would just work at the barn or the bar," she huffs.

"I know that I'm going to have to pick eventually," I say, pulling into the empty parking lot.

"If it's a money thing, you know I'm more than happy to help." I groan, and my mother laughs.

"Why are you so freaking stubborn?" she says. "Exactly like your father."

"Hey, I come from good stock," I say, and she goes soft. "I have to go, Mom. How about we have lunch this week?"

"I'll call you tomorrow," she says. "Love you, baby girl."

"Love you, too, Mom." I hang up the phone and look around the empty parking lot.

I'm surprised since Dolly is supposed to be here

already. I grab my phone and see that I don't have any messages from her. I get out of the truck and walk toward the entrance. The brown door has the name The Hideout painted blue on it. Unlocking the door with the keys I grabbed from my purse, I walk in and hear the alarm start to buzz. I punch in the code and look around.

It's exactly how I left it Saturday night when I left. One thing I did when I took over was close on Sunday. I made some small changes like adding a sports station with big screens so people can come in and watch the games. I have it totally closed off with its own bar and tables so it blocks the music.

I moved the bar from the wall to the center of the room in a big U. I made more barstools available, and I got me another bartender in, so the drinks flew out faster, which means they came back faster. I moved the dance floor all the way to the back of the house with a bigger stage for live music on Friday and Saturday nights.

I turn on the lights and walk toward the back office, my phone ringing. I pull it out of my back pocket and see Dolly's name.

"Hello," I say, walking into the little office. It has a desk and two chairs, the top of the desk totally organized.

"Amelia." I hear Dolly groaning, then coughing. "I've been up for the past two days. I have a fever and a terrible cough."

"Oh no, have you seen a doctor?" I ask, putting my purse in one of the chairs.

"I have an appointment tomorrow. I was hoping that I could pop some ibuprofen, but I just can't."

"No, of course not. Don't worry about it," I say, closing my eyes and worrying about it. "We'll be fine."

"I'm so sorry," she says and coughs again.

"It's perfect, okay? Get better and let me know what the doctor says." I hang up the phone and walk out, calling my other waitress, who doesn't answer.

The door opens, and I look up to see Jill walking in. "Happy Monday," she says, all chipper, and then she sees my face. "Why do you not look happy?"

"Dolly is sick," I say, and she stares at me. "It's just you and me, sugar," I say, and she rolls her eyes.

"Are there any big games tonight?" she asks, and I nod my head.

"We have two baseball games," I say, and she puts on a brave smile.

"It'll be fine. People can wait five more seconds for drinks," she says. "It's going to be fine."

"You know my rule," I say. "No one waits for a drink."

"Well, today they do, and you'll see that the world is not going to end," Jill says, walking into the sports area. "I'll take this bar. You take that bar, and people can come see us for drinks."

I close my eyes and try not to let it get to me. I walk to the bar and start setting it up. I know that if I call Chelsea, she would come in and help me, but I also know she didn't sleep last night and worked all day at the clinic.

I make sure I'm all set up, and we all have enough ice. I'm about to go and grab a couple of bottles from the back when the front door opens, and the construction guys start to pile in. They usually come here every

Monday and Friday to start and end the week.

"Howdy," I say to them as they walk in. Their shirts are dirty from working all day.

"Hey, Amelia," one of them says as they fill the stools at the bar.

"Where is Dolly?" another one asks me.

"She's sick," I tell them as I start filling drink orders. I work my way down the bar and look up, shocked to see more people than usual on a Monday night.

I see about ten guys come in and go straight into the sports room. I try to peek in to see if Jill needs help, but someone else comes to the bar to order.

I spot a couple of people come in and go straight to the billiard room. "I'll be right over," I tell them, and one of them holds up his hand with two fingers, so I know to bring them two beers.

I fill the orders and then rush back to bring them drinks when a table of girls signals me over to give me their mixed drinks order.

I get back behind the bar when I feel someone next to me. "Hey," Asher says, going to wash his hands. "What's going on here?"

"When did you get here?" I ask, shocked that he is drying his hands and then walking down the bar toward the end to grab the empty glasses and put them in the gray dirty bin.

"Thirty minutes ago," he says.

I finally look at him when he walks back to the end of the bar. "Um, what are you wearing?" I ask as I start to mix ice and tequila. I press the blender, and he looks over at me, and I notice how small his shirt is.

"This"—he points at his whole body—"is all Quinn's." I throw my head back and laugh. Turning and watching him, his black hair looks like he just ran his hand through it. His eyes are a soft brown but turn green when he's in the sun.

"It's a little bit of a tight fit," I say, and he looks over at me, and I wink at him. "How about you bring this to the girls so they can keep ordering drinks?"

He shakes his head. "Not on your life." He walks over to grab two shot glasses. "I walked in with them, and all I heard were cat noises," he says, and I place the drinks on the tray. "I'll make sure this is taken care of."

"Thank you," I say. Finally, at ten o'clock, the last person walks out, and I look over to see that he's wiping down the tables.

Jill comes over to me and hands me the black money bag. "Sports room is all clean."

"Thank you so much, Jill." I smile at her. "See you on Friday."

"I'm covering for Dolly tomorrow. She already called me," she says over her shoulder. "See you later."

I clean behind the bar, and when I look back up, Asher is taking the glasses to the back and setting them in the dishwasher. "I don't know if I can repay you," I say when he comes back out, and I finish counting the till. "This is for you." I hand him the white envelope.

"You arcn't paying me for tonight," he says, and I laugh.

"Good to know," I say. "But that is your share of the

tips." I move the envelope. "Come on, you earned it."

He shakes his head. "I owed you from today." I tilt my head to the side, confused. "You let me stay at your house."

"Oh, that?" I shake my head. "That wasn't a favor. After smelling you, it was …" I don't have to finish the sentace when he starts to laugh as he leans against the bar, and he looks exhausted. "How was today?"

"Exhausting," he answers.

"Where are you staying tonight?" I ask, and he looks down and then up.

"You don't have anywhere to stay."

"I was just going to stay in the truck," he answers honestly. I'm expecting him to argue with me and come up with an excuse. What I'm not expecting is what comes next. "Trust me, it's not the worst place I've ever slept." My heart shatters in my chest with just that one sentence.

Seven

Asher

THE WORDS LEAVE my mouth with a laugh, and I watch her eyes the whole time. I wait to see if she will look at me differently. Her eyes never leave mine, and they never change. "I've seen the inside of that truck." She shakes her head, and I have to literally catch my breath at her beauty. I noticed her the minute I started working at the farm. I also knew I wasn't going to disrespect the family by going after her. So I keep my distance and watch her from afar, hoping like fuck no one notices.

"When I was fifteen …" I want to slap my hand in front of my mouth to stop it from talking, but with her, all I want to do is to keep talking, just to be with her. "My foster brother, Ryan, and I found this couch in one of the alleys." I shake my head, thinking back to that time. "We had both decided that we were not going back to our foster home." I start to tap my finger on the bar. "We had seventeen dollars between us. God, we were such idiots."

"You were fifteen, and you thought you could live off seventeen dollars?" she asks, laughing and shaking her head. Her blue eyes light up. I can see she's tired, and I know I shouldn't keep her any longer than I am. She walks around the bar. Her black jeans mold to her hips, the blank tank top sticks to her small frame. "What happened?" she asks, pulling out a stool and hopping on it.

"We decided to spend the night resting. Hit the pavement the next day and start looking for jobs," I say.

"Well, at least you had a plan." She puts her hand up and leans her forehead on her fist.

"Oh, we had big plans," I say, climbing onto the stool next to her. "We were going to rule the world." I laugh, folding my hands together. "The night was hard. The honking, the sirens, the smell of urine … it was so gross." I look down at my hands. "But we were together and safe."

"Why do I feel like something is coming?" she asks with a twinkle in her eye.

"Oh, it came alright. The next day, we couldn't stop scratching." She gasps out and puts her hands in front of her mouth. "Turns out, the couch was full of bedbugs."

She claps her hands together. "Oh my God. What did you do?"

"Nothing." I shake my head, turning to her. "This

scar right here"—I point at a small scar right under my eye—"is from that."

"That is horrible," she says, and I shrug.

"Like I said, I've slept in worse places than the truck. I'll be fine," I say, getting up. "Let's go. It's getting late."

"Seriously, though," she says, not moving from her stool. "Why don't you just stay with me?"

"Because your family has helped me more than anyone else in my whole life," I say.

"What if it was me?" she asks, making me stop in my tracks. "Or anyone in my family? What if we lost everything we had, and you had this house with three bedrooms? Would you not offer it to us?"

"Of course, I would," I say, not skipping a beat.

"Good, so we got that covered. You can stay with me under one condition," she says, getting off the stool. "You never wear those jeans again."

I stand, folding my hand over my chest, knowing that I shouldn't take her up on her offer. I knew when I parked the truck in the parking lot tonight that I shouldn't come here. I knew when I walked in and saw her running back and forth that I should stay out of it. I knew all that, instead of following the yelling that was in my head. But what did I do? I jumped behind the bar and helped her out without thinking twice. "What are people going to say?"

Her eyebrows pinch together when she looks at me. "Well, they are going to think that I'm helping a friend out since you lived in our family barn that burned to the ground." She walks to the back of the bar toward the office.

"This is a horrible idea," I say to myself. "Just leave and say no," I say, knowing full well I would never leave her to walk to her car by herself in the dark.

"Okay, I'm ready to go," she says, coming back with her purse in her hand.

I wait for her to walk toward the door before I walk behind her. She sets the alarm and turns off the light, taking one look back at the bar and smiling. We walk out, and the dark air is still. "Is it always this dark?" I ask, and she looks around.

"No," she says and looks up to see two of the spotlights are off. "Fuck, I need to change the lights."

"I'll do it tomorrow," I say, and she grabs her phone out of her pocket. "What are you doing?"

"Making a note so I don't forget," she says.

"I just told you I'm going to do it," I say, and she ignores me and starts to walk toward her car. "Why are you like that?" I ask her when she stops right beside her car, folding my arms over my chest.

"I don't know," she huffs out. "Why are you like you are?" she throws back at me, going to her purse to fish out her keys. "Why don't you accept help when you are given it?"

"You are a pain in the ass," I finally say, instead of saying she is right.

"Well, good news, then." She presses the button to open her car door. "I take it you will be coming to sleep in a bed tonight instead of a back seat?"

"Do I have a choice?" I ask, reaching out to open her

door.

"We all have choices, Asher," she says, standing in front of me. "You have a choice to be an idiot and sleep in the back of your truck …" She tilts her head to the side, and even in the dark of the night, I can see the crystal in her eyes. "Or you can take me up on my offer and sleep in a bed that does not have bedbugs but that has been thrown up on and cleaned."

I laugh at her. "Well, when you put it that way, how can I say no to a bed that once had vomit on it?"

"Good choice," she says. "I'm going to pick up food on the way home. If you get there before me, the garage code is one, two, three, four."

"Your garage door is one, two, three, four?" I ask, shocked. "Your uncle is Casey Barnes, and you have one, two, three, four as a fucking code?"

She rolls her eyes at me. "You can change it if you like." She reaches out and grabs the door handle. I help her close the door, and I stand here, watching the car drive away.

Shaking my head, I grab the phone out of my pocket and walk back to the door of the bar. I turn on the flashlight and point it toward the spotlights that are out and I see that there is a hole in one of them. I look down at the ground and see the small pieces of glass on the ground. I snap a picture of the light and then walk over to the other one. I can't see anything wrong with it.

I walk back to my truck and feel eyes on me. I turn around with my flashlight from my phone looking around. "Hello," I say to no one. I turn from one side to

NATASHA MADISON

the next seeing no one there, but still feeling eyes on me.

I look at the clock and see that it's almost eleven and I don't know who is up. Instead, I send a text to Ethan, Casey, and Jacob.

Me: There is one busted light at the bar. Is there a camera feed?

My phone rings in my hand. I look down and see that it's Jacob.

"Hey." I start my truck now.

"What do you mean the lights are busted?" Jacob asks right away, and I can hear rustling in the background.

"I was walking Amelia out of the bar, and I realized it was pitch black. She thought the lights were out, but when I went back and checked, I saw one busted. I can't see the other one in the dark, but I'm going to come by tomorrow and change it."

"I told Beau that he should get cameras up," he says. "I'm going to call Casey tomorrow to see."

"While you are doing that, you should know that her garage password is one, two, three, four," I say, and he hisses out and groans.

"I thought she was joking," he says. "That kid is her mother's daughter."

I smile because as much as I want to agree with him, I see a lot more of Jacob in her than I do Kallie. But I only know Kallie from a handful of times I've seen her at the barbecue. "Where are you staying tonight?" he asks, and my stomach burns when I think of the answer.

"I was going to stay in the truck," I say, "but Amelia

said I could stay in her spare bedroom."

"If you don't want to stay there," he says, "you can always come and stay with us."

I look down, the heat rising in my neck, and my stomach rises and falls. "You don't have to do that."

"Please," he says. "Listen, Asher, I know you've just come into town, and I know you have a great job and position at the farm," he says, "but I'd like to talk to you about your options."

"My options?" I repeat the words, not sure what he means by this.

"You ever think of going into law enforcement?" he asks, and I tap the steering wheel. "I'd love to sit down with you and talk to you more about it."

"I …" I say. "I'd like that."

"Good," he says. "I'll call you tomorrow to set up a time and place."

"Sounds good," I say and disconnect.

I need to grab my shit and leave, my head screams to me. *I can't stay here. It's not right.*

I close my eyes and put my head back. The phone in my hand vibrates, and when I look down, I see a text from Amelia.

Amelia: Got you a burger. It's in the microwave. Good night.

"This is not good." I make my way over to her house even though I know I shouldn't.

Eight

AMELIA

THE SMELL OF bacon makes me open one eye, and I think I'm dreaming. I'm on my side in the middle of my bed with four pillows all around me and the cover up to my eyes. I turn and slip my hand out of the hot cocoon, grabbing my phone and seeing it's only six o'clock.

I groan and put my hands back under the cover and close my eyes. Why does it smell like bacon? I look over at my closed door and smell coffee. What the hell is going on right now? Is my mother here? My head is asking me all these questions, and I know I'm not going to fall back asleep and get those extra forty-five minutes.

Throwing the cover off me, I get up and see the sun is starting to come up. I walk into the kitchen, and I have to close one eye when I see all the lights on. Asher's naked back is to me as he stands in front of the stove. "What the hell are you doing?" I ask, standing in the hallway that leads to the kitchen from my bedroom. "It's six o'clock."

He looks over his shoulder, and I wish he really wouldn't. His face has that sleepiness still on it, and his hair is sticking up in certain places, and his smirk just makes my stomach sink. This is not good. I should never have told him to come home with me. I mean, I didn't really tell him to come with me. I told him he could use my guest bedroom, so there is a difference there. "I'm making you breakfast," he says, grabbing a cup of coffee from beside him on the counter and bringing it to his mouth. "The coffee is ready."

"Why?" It's the only thing that can come to my mind, and he turns around and leans against the counter. I see his six-pack is on point, and I wonder what it would be like to be held by him. I picture it so clearly in my head, his arms around mine as I look up at him. It's a picture I quickly erase before I give it a second thought. "Why are you cooking me breakfast at the ass crack of dawn?"

He chuckles. "I'm going to say you aren't a morning person." His smirk irritates me. Not because I don't like it but because I like it too fucking much.

"I'm a morning person," I lie to him. I have never been a morning person in my whole life. You can only talk to me after at least one cup of coffee, and one must ease into it. It's why Quinn makes me start at eight instead of seven. I fold my arms over my chest. "I just don't get the whole *cooking at six o'clock* thing." My feet move on their own as I walk into the kitchen and see the bacon cooking in the cast-iron pan. "Like the sun isn't even up completely yet." I grab a coffee cup and walk over to the pot, pouring myself a cup. I bring it to my nose and smell it. "Nothing like the smell of coffee in the morning," I say, taking a sip of the hot coffee.

"You drink it black?" he asks, grabbing the fork and flipping the bacon over.

"Yeah, I ran out of milk one day, and well, it just stuck," I say. "Besides, that means I never have to be disappointed." I take another sip.

"How do you like your eggs?" he asks, and I look at him.

"Cooked." I laugh at my own joke, and he fake laughs, walking to my fridge and taking out the eggs. The way he does it makes it seem as if he's been doing this for a long time. I don't know why this bothers me so much. The last thing I want is to expect him to do it for me. Did that once and never going to do that again.

I learned a while ago that you can never count on anyone but yourself. I've also learned to never expect anyone to do anything for you. "You don't have to do all of this." I point at the stove, and I suddenly get a whiff of something baking. "What's in the oven?"

"You had some biscuits in the freezer," he says, opening the oven, and I can see they are golden and almost ready. "It's the least I could do. Not only did you give me a place to sleep but you also bought me dinner."

"That's where you are wrong." I point at him. "I picked up dinner for myself and bought you one because you busted your ass for me."

"You can spin it any way you want to," he says, grabbing the empty plate beside him with paper towels on it. He places the bacon in the middle of the plate and turns back to grab another pan to do the eggs in. "The fact is you did me a huge favor last night, actually all day, and this is the only way I know to repay you."

I can think of something else you can do, my head says, and I bring the cup to my mouth to make sure I don't vocalize that thought. "Well, I guess I should say thank you." He just nods his head. "Where did you learn to cook?" I could go and sit down on one of the stools at the island. I could sit at the table, but instead, I choose to stand beside him as he leans against the counter, listening to him talk.

"When I turned sixteen, I was hired as a busboy for a small diner," he says, cracking the eggs in a bowl. "Busboy soon turned to cook when he showed up and was drunk." He shakes his head. He comes over, grabbing my hip as he reaches for a paper towel. My hip feels like it's been scorched by his touch.

"Really?" I ask, and I find myself always entranced by his stories. I always want more. I could sit and listen to his stories for hours. Last night I was dead tired to the bone, but I sat down, and I wanted to hear more of the story. I wanted to ask him what he did after that. I wanted to ask him where he slept the next day. I wanted to know it all, and that fact in itself scared me straight to my core.

"Yeah, he stumbled in there," he says, adding milk to the eggs, "and then fell on his ass when he walked into the kitchen." He laughs. "I was shocked because he was a big man, but instead of getting up, he lay there in the middle of the kitchen snoring." He opens the drawers, looking for something; I watch the muscles in his arm flex every time he pulls a drawer out.

I'm like a fucking schoolgirl. I avoid looking at him and look out the window to see that the sun has officially risen. Two birds fly together into the trees. "No one knew what to do." I turn back to Asher and see him whisking the eggs. "Waitress asked me if I knew how to cook eggs. I lied and said yes." He pours the eggs into the pan and slowly whisks them. "I had no fucking idea how to cook shit. The most I knew how to do was pour water into a ramen cup." He takes his time whisking. "So I learned pretty fast, and apparently, the eggs were not horrible, so they hired me to be the morning cook."

"Why did you stop?" I ask, and he looks over at me.

"The diner wasn't in the best part of the city, and the dealers would use it as their office at night. There was a drive-by shooting, and well, when I went back in the morning, nothing was left."

My mouth hangs in shock. "You could have died?" I say, and he just shrugs.

"If it's my time to go, it's my time to go regardless of where I am," he says as he turns to get the oven mitt. He opens the oven and takes out the pan of biscuits. He put the hot tray on top of the stove. "It could have happened at five a.m. instead of eleven p.m." He grabs two plates. "The good thing is that I was able to get a job not too long after in the kitchen." He smiles. "So everything worked out."

I watch him place two scoops of fluffy eggs onto a plate and then place two slices of bacon with two biscuits side by side. "Do you want more?" he asks, holding the plate in front of me.

"No." I shake my head, grabbing the plate and bringing it to my nose. My fingers tingle from his hands brushing against mine.

"You smell everything." He laughs at me, and I look at him. "You don't notice it."

"No." I shake my head, and I look at him, trying not to let it show that I'm shocked he noticed. No one in my whole life has ever noticed that I do that.

"You got up, and you smelled your coffee." He turns to plate his own eggs and bacon, leaving two more pieces on the plate. I put my plate down and grab the extra slices and place them on his plate.

"Who doesn't smell coffee first thing in the morning?" I counter him. Turning to refill my coffee cup, I walk to his and top his off as well. I ignore the fact that his eyes are watching me. I look over at him when I grab two forks out of the drawer. "Everyone smells their coffee."

"Okay, but they don't smell the flowers when they walk into work. Nor do they look up and smell the sky when they get out of their car." I stop moving, trying not to overthink that he watches me when I get to work.

"I have your fork," I say softly, turning to grab my cup and walking to the table. I sit in the chair I always sit in, and he sits down in front of me. "Thank you for making breakfast," I mumble, not making eye contact with him. "You didn't have to."

"I know I didn't have to," he says, and I can feel that his eyes are on me. "But I wanted to," he says, and I don't bother looking at him.

I grab my fork and taste the eggs; the buttery fluffy eggs melt on my tongue. "These are good," I say, still not looking up at him. He doesn't say anything to me as we eat, and when he gets up to put his plate in the dishwasher, I turn and look at him. "I'll clean up." He looks over at me. "You cooked, I clean. It's a universal law." I try to make a joke out of it and look over to see that it's almost seven and I know he starts at seven. "You better get going; you start in ten minutes."

He turns the water off and dries his hands. "I guess I'll see you later," he says, and I watch his back retreating and he stops and turns back to look at me. "I'm sorry if I said something that offended you in any way."

"You didn't," I tell him. "This was lovely," I say, and he just nods and turns to walk back into the bedroom. I sit here at the table and I know that I should leave before he comes back out. I put the plate in the sink and walk back to my bedroom.

I close my door softly behind me and put my back on it, leaning my head back. The sounds of him walking around have me looking out the window to see him leaving with the black bag.

"It's for the best," I say out loud. "You have one goal and one goal only," I remind myself. "And being stupid and in love is not one of those goals."

Nine

Asher

I CARRY THE bag out with me, because no matter how much I want to go back, I'm not going to. I toss the bag in the back seat and get into the truck. The heat already starting to feel thick, I drive toward Casey's headquarters, not surprised when I see Ethan's car already there.

You would never know that in this white tin barn holds the most advanced computer technology in the world. Casey isn't just a cowboy, he's a computer tech.

Getting out of the truck, I pull open the door and come face-to-face with a white room with a desk. No one is behind it. I knock on the closed white metal door and the buzzing starts, I pull open the door and step inside what I call the "war" room.

The whole back wall is filled with five big screens

side by side. Five desks are on each side of the room with full computers on them. The screens in front come to this big square table that sits in front of the big screens. There are screens built into the desk and it's all touch screen. "Good morning," Ethan says, standing there wearing jeans and a shirt with a cup of coffee in his hand. "I see we went shopping for clothes that fit you." He tries to hide the laugh with his cup.

"Yeah." I look down at the blue jeans and white shirt I picked up yesterday before going to the bar.

"You want coffee?" he asks, walking over to one of the desks and sitting down.

"No, I just had two cups with breakfast," I say and I want to kick myself when his eyebrows pinch together.

"I was at the diner this morning with my father and I didn't see you there," he says, leaning back in his chair.

"Yeah, I stayed with Amelia. Helped her at the bar last night and she offered me her guest room." I make sure there is nothing in my tone that would make him suspicious even though there was nothing to be suspicious about. "Made breakfast to thank her."

"Did you give her coffee before you spoke to her?" he asks. "She is not a morning person. I remember once we were teasing her and she tried to stab my hand with her fork."

I laugh thinking about how cranky she was but not knowing that she needed coffee before I spoke to her. "She had coffee."

"Good." He brings his cup of coffee to his mouth and takes a sip. "Got your text. My father and I rode out there this morning before I came here. One definitely looks like someone broke it. We looked around a bit, but we didn't see anything strange."

"I'm going to run over there this afternoon and change the lights out," I say, and he nods.

"My father put in an order to put up cameras," Ethan says. "We just didn't tell Amelia yet." I shake my head. The woman has to be the most stubborn woman I've ever met. But then again, she is the most interesting also. She is smart and kind and hardworking and fiercely independent. Everything about her intrigues me and I want to ask her so many questions. "He's going to swing by today and break it to her."

"Or you do it during the day when she isn't there and then see how long it takes for her to notice," I say, and he taps his coffee cup thinking about it.

"We could and then just blame it on my father." He gets up and grabs his phone. "She can't hurt him."

"Okay, if you need me, call," I say, walking out of the room and getting into the truck.

I do everything I need to do for the barn before grabbing the ladder and making my way over to the bar. It's almost four thirty when I pull up. I see her car parked there next to another one. Pulling up as close as I can to the door, I get out and unload the ladder and the lights. I place the ladder against the building and the door opens.

I look toward her and everything inside me stops. I haven't seen her since this morning and she stands there with her blue jeans and white tank top. Her hair is braided on the side, her eyes a crystal blue. So blue you can drown in them and die happy. "Hey." She smiles at me. "I was wondering who was out here."

"I'm going to change the lights." I point up toward the lights. My palms are getting sweaty as my heart beats faster and faster in my chest. "I was going to come out here earlier, but we had to round up a couple of cows that got loose and I had to help your grandfather."

"That's okay," she says. "Tuesdays are usually quiet and we don't have any games on today." She walks over to stand beside me. "How can I help?"

"You can go back inside," I say, grabbing the lights and walking toward the ladder.

"I can hand you the lights," she says, grabbing them out of my hands. "And I'll forget you just said that the next time I pour you a drink." She smiles at me and I can tell it's a *fuck you* smile.

I laugh. "Fine." Knowing even if I fight with her, she is just going to do what she wants to do. I climb the ladder, seeing up close that someone must have broken the light with a rock. "Can you go into the truck and get me a rag?"

"Oh, you need me?" she asks, looking up at me, her hand on her forehead blocking out the sun. "It's a good thing I didn't go inside." She turns on her boots and walks toward the truck, opening the back door and grabbing the T-shirt Quinn lent me.

"I said a rag," I say, and she tosses me the shirt.

"Are you going to actually wear that shirt again?" she asks me.

"No, but I was going to give it back to him," I inform

Southern secrets

her, holding the shirt in my hand.

"Trust me, he doesn't want it back," she says, putting one boot on the last step of the ladder. "No way he can ever wear that shirt. He'll look like a skinny boy in it."

I look down at her. "You were checking me out?" I joke with her.

"Everyone and their mother was checking you out," she says. "Even the guys checked out your package."

"It wasn't that bad," I say, and I know it was that bad because I had to pull the seam out of my balls at least ten times. I use the shirt to unscrew the light bulb. I'm about to go down when I feel her stepping on the second step stretching her hand up with the new light.

"Here, take this and give me the old one," she says. We exchange the bulbs and I screw in the new one.

I walk down the ladder and look at her. "You can't just let someone do something for you." I don't know if I'm so much as asking her as if I'm telling her.

"It's not that I can't let anyone do anything for me," she says, putting the broken light away. "If I can help, why wouldn't I?" She grabs the new bulb as I move the ladder over to the other light. Going up and seeing that this one, too, has been busted, I take out my phone and take a picture of it before I take it out and replace it.

"You want to go inside and open the lights and see if they work?" I ask as some trucks arrive. The sound of gravel making me look toward the trucks.

I grab my phone and send the text to Jacob.

Me: Just changed the lights and they were both busted with rocks.

I press send and look up when I see a couple of guys from the barn. "Hey." I nod to a couple of them.

"You coming to have a beer with us?" Elliot, one of the foremen, asks me. "My treat."

"Yeah, I'll be right in," I say, putting the ladder in the back of my truck.

The phone pings in my pocket and I take it out to see it's a text from Jacob.

Jacob: We are installing cameras tomorrow. She will just have to deal with it.

I shake my head and answer him back.

Me: Good luck with that.

I put my phone away and walk into the bar. I see that it's quieter than it was yesterday. I spot Amelia in back of the bar as she is pouring a beer in a glass. Walking to the back I go to the bathroom and wash my hands.

"You should go and get a motel room," my head tells me when I look at my reflection.

Drying my hands, I don't look at myself in the mirror before I walk out. I join the guys at the bar and sit on the empty stool. "What can I get you?" Amelia asks when she comes to me.

"I don't know. If I ask for a beer, will you put something inside it?" I ask, and she throws her head back and laughs. Her neck is bare, and I close my eyes and picture myself biting her and leaving my mark. My cock springs to action wanting in on the picture.

She doesn't answer me. Instead, she walks down to the beer taps as she fills a glass for me. She puts a coaster down and places the beer on it. "There you go," she says and smiles. "It's safe to drink." She turns and walks away, and I want to ask her to come back and talk to me.

Instead, I just take the beer and take a sip. The guys finish their beer and head out to their house. I am the only one at the bar. "It really is quiet on Tuesday," I say, and she nods her head, as she wipes down the bar where the guys left. I look over seeing that it's almost nine o'clock and the bar is empty.

"Why do you do it?" I finally ask her the question I've been thinking about all day. My thumb is hitting the top of the wooden bar.

"Why do I do what?" she asks, looking at me.

"Work the two jobs." She looks at me.

"Well, for one, I have bills," she says. "And I'm paying my aunt monthly to own this."

"You bought the bar?" I ask, shocked when she nods her head. "Yeah."

"I knew you were independent and hard-working," I say, and she looks at me. "But I had no idea that you were working to buy the bar."

"Yeah," she says, and I know she is hiding something. I can feel it. "She wanted to just give me the bar," she says as Jill comes out of the sports section.

"Hey, it's all done. Do you think I can clock out?" she asks Amelia, who nods her head.

"I'm going to close up, too." She looks at the clock on the wall. "See you Thursday," she says, and Jill turns to walk out of the place. I get off the stool and walk around the bar.

"What are you doing?" she asks, shocked.

"Well, it'll go faster if we both do this," I say as I grab the dirty glasses.

"First breakfast and now this." She smirks at me. "You don't have to keep doing this to stay with me." My eyebrows pinch together. "All you have to do is pick up after yourself." She turns around and walks toward the office, leaving me with my mouth hanging open.

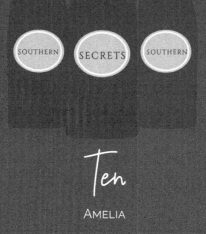

Ten

AMELIA

WHY THE FUCK did you just invite him to come over again? I yell at myself when I walk into the office. I place the money in the safe and turn back to walk out. It takes us ten minutes to close everything since tonight was abnormally quieter than usual. "Thank you," I say when I lock the door. I start walking to my car and look up at the lights he changed. "For the lights and helping me clean up."

"My pleasure," he says and stops by my car as I grab the keys. I unlock the door, and he opens the door for me.

"I'm going to grab something to eat," he says. "Want me to grab something for you?"

NO, my head screams. "Yeah, that sounds good." *Fucking hell*, I curse myself.

"Perfect, I'll see you soon," he says, waiting for me to get in the car. I get in and pull away from the bar without looking in the rearview mirror. I storm into the house, kicking off my boots and then going to the bathroom.

I start the shower, hoping that when I get out, he'll be asleep, and I can eat without him pushing my buttons. I spend too long in the shower on purpose, and when I walk out to the kitchen, I stop in my tracks as I see him leaning on the island with the bag of food beside him. "Did you not eat?" I ask, and he looks up.

"No, I was waiting for you," he says, standing up and putting his phone down. "I didn't know what you wanted, so I got you," he says, taking the sandwiches out of the bag. "Grilled and fried."

"Oh my God," I say, the towel that is piled on my hair falling off. "Um, I guess I'll take the chicken." I look at him. "Grilled."

"Okay," he says, handing me the sandwich and then grabs the other one.

"Did you not order anything for yourself?" I ask, walking to the island.

"I figured I would eat what you didn't want," he says. "It doesn't matter to me as long as it's food." I ignore the fact that he didn't pick first and let me choose. I ignore that no one has done that for me.

"Okay, I guess this is a good time to talk about things." I open the sandwich and take a bite before turning and walking to grab a glass. "Until you get a place to stay, why don't you stay here?"

"I don't know," he answers, eating the other sandwich.

"Is it going to be weird?"

"No," I answer honestly. "I'm assuming you aren't going to treat my house like a revolving door."

"What does that mean?" he asks, grabbing a glass and pouring himself something to drink.

"You aren't going to parade women in and out of my house," I say, and his hand stops midway to his mouth. "Other than that, I think it'll be fine."

"So the only thing you have a problem with is me having sex with other women?" he asks me and tries to hide the smirk by bringing the glass to his mouth.

"No." I ignore the pull to look in his eyes. "I have a problem with you bringing the women here to have sex."

"One," he says. "For the record, I would never disrespect you like that."

"Good to know," I say, ignoring the burning in my stomach. He didn't say he wouldn't have sex with other women. He just said he won't do it here.

"I take it you don't date," he says, and I finally look up at him.

"There is no time in my life to start dating," I say. "I worry about one person and one person only. Me." He just stares at me. I don't add anything else to it because there is no need to. No one needs to know what I went through. I won't even tell Chelsea, so the last thing I'm going to do is tell Asher.

"It'll happen when it's meant to happen," he says, and I just nod at him. "You ever fall in love?"

I think about my answer. I think about lying about it. "Yup," I say. "Long time ago. Found out it wasn't for me." I look down and blink away the one tear that threatens to fall. I will not shed one tear for him. "What about you?"

He laughs. "Yeah, because everyone wants to fall in love with a homeless kid who lives paycheck to paycheck and had to work three jobs at one time because the only person he's ever had stand by his side got sick and needed meds. In the end, nothing could save him, and he died." He shakes his head as I see him blink away tears. My hand flies out to touch his arm, and my thumb rubs his warm skin. "No, I've never been in love." I don't move my hand, and his eyes go to my hand on his arm.

He walks away from me, my hand falling onto the counter. "Love, it's a strange thing," I say, breaking the silence. He throws away his wrapper and looks over at me.

"If you say so," he says and walks toward the bedroom. "Thank you for letting me stay with you, Amelia." He looks down. "I'll be out of your hair before you know it."

I just nod my head at him and watch him walk toward the bedroom. He closes the door softly behind him, and I want to go and ask him all the questions, but what right do I have. No right, because if he asked me, I don't know if I would answer him.

Turning off the lights, I walk to my bedroom and slip into bed. I close my eyes, and usually I can fall asleep right away, but tonight, I hear his voice in my head. *Have you ever been in love?* The loaded question still hurts me to this day. I let the tear run down to my pillow as I fight back the memories that come with it.

That night, I dream about what could have been. What was supposed to be, but when I grab my husband's hand, it's Asher's face that is there.

My eyes fly open, and I stay in bed until I hear him walk out the front door. When I walk into the kitchen, I spot the plate on the stove with a note on it. I pick up the white paper, reading what he left.

Didn't want to wake you.

See you later.

A

I bring the note to my nose, seeing if it smells like him and then look around to see if he isn't standing there watching me. I look over to see the coffee pot still on. Grabbing a cup of coffee, I eat, standing at the island.

I don't see him that day, nor does he show up at the bar that night. I push the disappointment away from myself, and when I park in the driveway, his truck is there. When I walk in, I'm expecting to see him in the kitchen. The only thing that greets me is the soft light coming from the stovetop.

I toss my keys on the counter and walk to the stove, seeing a plate there with another note.

Your grandmother sent this for you.

A

I look toward the guest bedroom. The door is closed, and the light off. I warm the food and take it to my bedroom with me.

The next morning, I wake up early, and even though I won't admit it to myself, I walk out and see that he isn't there. The coffee is started, but no food. I grab a cup and walk back into my room.

What is your problem? I ask myself, and I want to yell that this is what I wanted. The disappointment running through me makes my stomach burn and my heart ache just a tiny bit. I fight it back, reminding myself this is all for the best.

Getting to the barn, I say hello to everyone as I go to my desk. I walk back to the stalls to see if Willow or Quinn is there. When I don't spot either of them, I take my phone out, and I'm about to call them when I hear a car door shut. My heart speeds up, my palms get sweaty, and my mouth suddenly goes dry.

I walk toward the barn door, and when I see that it's my mother, this sudden letdown runs through me. "There is my girl," my mother says, smiling when she sees me. Walking to the passenger side of the truck, she opens it and grabs two white bags.

"Let me help you." I rush to her and grab a heavy bag from her.

"Thank you," she says, and she puts her arm around me as we walk back into the barn. "You look tired."

"I'm not," I answer her honestly. "What is all this?" I change the subject.

"That is for Asher," she says, and I want to roll my eyes. "He was at your grandparents' yesterday, and your grandmother went on a shopping spree."

"He can buy his own clothes," I huff, walking to my car to dump the bags in there.

"What are you doing?" my mother asks me.

"I'll bring them home to Asher," I say, and her

eyebrows shoot up.

"Wait, he's staying with you?" she asks me when I grab the bag from her hand and dump it into the back seat of my car.

"Yeah," I say, avoiding her eyes and closing the car door. "He helped me out."

"Is that a good idea?" my mother asks me softly.

"Why wouldn't it be a good idea?" I fold my arms over my chest. "He needs help. What was I supposed to do?"

"Have you had coffee today?" my mother asks, trying to hide the sly smile.

"I'm fine," I say, annoyed. "I'm not tired. I'm helping a friend, and it's fine."

She walks to me and puts her hand on my cheek, and I look at her. She looks the same she did when she was eighteen. "One of these days, someone is going to want to help you juggle all those balls you have in the air, and you are going to freak the fuck out."

"Mom!" I laugh. "You just said the f-word." I point at her.

"Damn straight, I did," she says. "Now, what is troubling you?"

"Nothing," I say, trying to figure it out myself. "I'm cranky, and I don't know why, and it's bothering me that I can't fix why I'm cranky."

"Unless you know the answer and you don't like it," my mother says, and it makes me put my head back and groan. "I have to get back to work." She kisses my cheek. "I'll see you Sunday, yes?"

"Always," I say and watch her get into her truck and pull off.

I grab my phone and pull up Asher's name. Going to the text.

Me: Where have you been?

I quickly delete it and start again.

Me: Haven't seen you in a while.

I erase that also. "What the fuck?" I mumble.

Me: My mother dropped off clothes. Come and get them.

I stare at it for a good ten seconds before I delete it.

Me: My mother dropped off clothes for you. I'll leave them at home.

I press send before I erase it and put my phone away, turning when the hair on the back of my neck flies up, and I feel someone watching me. I turn in a circle and look at the open field toward the dense bushes in the back. I see what looks like a little orange circle, and when I pick up my hand to put it over my eyes to see better, I can't find it again.

Eleven

Asher

I GET OUT of the truck after having to park almost in the street. I can hear the country music all the way over here. The parking lot is jam-packed as I see the lights coming out from the windows. The walk to the bar is the longest, and even though I told myself coming here wasn't a good idea, I still got dressed, and here I am.

The whole week I've avoided seeing her. I mean, not that I had the time not to avoid her. I spent the week helping Billy repair fences. The man was doing it himself when I found him. When I got home, I had enough energy for a shower. I fell asleep, but I would listen for her and only fully fall asleep when I heard her come in.

In the morning, I tried to make the least amount of noise I could so I didn't wake her. But I was hoping she would come out. The only thing I've heard from her is a text about the clothes her grandmother bought me.

I pull open the door, and the heat from all the people in there hits me right away. I take one step in and stop in awe. The bar is jam-packed. I mean, it usually is on a Saturday, but it's more so today. All you see is a sea of people. I move through the crowd toward the bar and stop when I see Ethan and Emily standing by a table talking.

"Hey," I say to them and look around. "This is crazy."

"Yeah, my sister got one of the popular bands to come and play tonight," Ethan says, looking around and smiling. "She should have charged a cover."

"Nah," I say, looking around and seeing that people are crowded on the dance floor, and the band hasn't even started yet. "This is better. They will buy drinks instead of paying for the cover."

"Exactly what she said to us." Emily smiles and steps closer to Ethan when someone tries to walk past her.

I take a second to look over at the pool tables part of the bar and see at least forty people around the two tables. I look toward the sports section and see the door opening and closing every second as someone goes in and leaves. I can tell that even that part of the bar is jam-packed, but there are some games on tonight. I do know that some of the men who come with their wives or girlfriends leave them to dance and go watch the game. Something for everyone.

"Are you here with anyone?" Emily asks, and I look at her.

"Not that I know of," I say, laughing. "I'm going to go get something to drink. You guys want something?"

"A beer," Ethan says right away, and someone bumps into Emily, pushing her into him. She smiles at him as she wraps an arm around his shoulder.

"I'm good," Emily says, and they share a smile, and he bends to kiss her. I walk away from them and zigzag my way toward the bar.

I can't even get close enough to order, but I'm close enough to see her. She throws her head back at something and laughs. Her hair is down today, and she curled the ends, parting it down the middle. Her eyes shine so blue they look crystal from here. She is wearing a green tank top with a black vest, showing off her tanned, toned arms. She holds her hand up, pointing at someone to grab their drink order.

She turns, and I see it's just her and someone else behind the bar, which is unusual on a Saturday. Usually, she has three people. *She doesn't need your help*, my head screams at me at the same time as my feet move to the side.

"Excuse me," I say as I make my way around the bar, and I stop when I see she's wearing jean shorts with a thick brown cowboy belt. Her long, lean, tanned legs are fully exposed with short cowboy boots. My heart goes up to my throat as I watch her walking back to the guy and getting the money from him.

She turns around, and she sees me and stops moving, my feet walking toward her. "Hey," she says, a smile filling her face, and the heart that has risen to my throat feels like it's going to come out. "Fancy seeing you here, roomie."

"Figured this was the only place I could see you," I finally say. "I'm assuming if I try to offer you help, you will say no." She rolls her eyes. "That's what I thought."

"Fine," she admits. "A bit more people are here than I thought would be," she says, looking toward the crowd, then turning back and smiling big. "But it's so fucking awesome," she says, clapping her hands over her head. "Now let's get the drinks flowing."

I've never seen her this happy. Usually, she reserves her happiness and doesn't really let it show.

"Who hasn't been served?" I ask the crowd, and we work side by side. I spend more time than I want to looking over at her as she works the crowd. I look to the side and see Ethan.

"Where the fuck is my beer?" he asks, and it's my turn to laugh as I turn, going to grab a glass at the same time Amelia does. She looks at me, and for one second, all the noise in the whole place is suddenly quiet.

"Take it," I say, and she grabs the glass and turns, and all I can do is smell her. I blink twice, turning and standing next to her while I prepare Ethan's beer.

"Ethan doesn't pay," she says, "and if he gives you money and you take it, I will shove my boot up your ass."

"Why do I get a boot up my ass if he doesn't listen?" I laugh, looking at her, and she just shrugs, putting down the beer and snapping her finger to take another order.

"I was told," I say to Ethan, handing him his beer,

"that if you give me money, she is going to shove her boot up *my* ass." I turn, going to grab a water bottle.

Ethan laughs when I hand him the bottle. "That's okay," he says. "I usually go and pay at the sports bar." My mouth goes open wide in shock. "Or I leave it in her tip jar when she isn't watching."

"So stubbornness runs in the family?" I ask, and he laughs.

"You tell me." He takes a sip of his beer. "You tried telling my grandfather that he needed to watch you do all the work. How did that go?"

I shake my head. "He tried to take out a wooden post the other day without batting an eye." Working side by side with Billy was an experience I will always remember and is up there on the top five best things that ever happened to me, and so far, I only have three.

"Let me know if you need anything else," I say and turn to go back to serving people.

I turn and see a group of six girls sitting at the end of the bar. "What can I get you?" I stretch my arms on the side and hold on to the bar.

"That is a loaded question," one of the blondes says, leaning into the bar. Her top is riding just a touch too low. "What's your specialty?"

"Beer," I say, and she laughs while the brunette cuts in.

"I'll have a beer with a blowjob on the side." She winks at me, and my face almost grimaces.

"Oh, I'll do a blowjob also," the other blonde says.

"Six blowjobs," the blonde says. "I'm Amanda."

I force a smile on my face. "I'll be right back." Turning and grabbing six shot glasses, I line them up in front of them. I walk over to Amelia, who is pouring a whiskey. "Do you have whipped cream?" I ask, and she looks over at me.

"Does this look like a place that has whipped cream?" She laughs. "Why?"

"They want blowjob shots." I motion with my head toward the girls. She throws her head back and laughs.

"Like those girls swallow." She laughs, and for the second time tonight, I'm left speechless.

"That's a no, then," I say, trying to hide my smirk.

"They are just going to have to swallow without the cream." She smiles sweetly.

"Okay, boss." I grab the Baileys and go back to the glasses. "Ladies, no whipped cream." I look at them. "Do you still want them?"

"Sure," the brunette says. I pour the Kahlua first and then top it with Baileys. "Aren't you doing a shot with us?"

"I can't drink on the job," I say. "That'll be thirty dollars."

The blonde takes a fifty out of her purse. "Keep the change." I nod my head and turn around, putting the money in the till.

"Twenty-dollar tip for six shots?" Amelia asks when I put a twenty in the tip jar, and I ignore her.

"Guess they have money to spare." I look over and serve two more ladies who smile at me.

"Cowboy," the blonde from before calls me over. I

don't want to go, and I almost ask Amelia to take my place, but she's serving drinks at the other end.

"What can I get you guys?" I ask, and the blonde leans onto the bar.

"You're a cowboy, right?" she asks, and I tilt my head, reminding myself that if I'm rude, then they won't come back, and if they don't come back, Amelia makes less money.

"Why do you think I'm a cowboy?" I ask.

"Well, for one, you're hot," the brunette says. "And your arms are nice and tanned."

"If you live around here or work around here, you're a cowboy," one of the other girls says. "I'll take a whiskey sour." I look at the other girls, who nod. "Six whiskey sours." I make their drinks in front of them and collect the money. I learned a long time ago never to leave someone with a tab running unless you know where they live.

"So tell us, Cowboy, do you have a name?" the blonde asks me again.

"Cowboy is good," I say and try to move away from her when she puts her hand on mine. I look down at her hand on mine and then hear someone clear their throat beside me.

"Sorry, I need the whiskey," Amelia says, and I move out of the way and out of reach from the blonde.

She grabs the bottle from the bar and then looks at me. "We got this covered," she says. "You can go and sit with your friends." She motions with her chin, and I just stare at her when she turns and walks away from me.

SOUTHERN SECRETS SOUTHERN

Twelve

Amelia

"WE GOT THIS covered," I say, irritated with myself for caring that those women were throwing themselves at him. "You can go and sit with your friends." I motion with my chin toward the girls who look like they are dry humping my bar.

I turn to walk away from him, and I'm stopped when he puts his hand on my arm. I look down, seeing his fingers wrapped around my upper arm. I look over at him and the lump in my throat suddenly appears.

I haven't seen him all week long, and even if I didn't want to admit it, it bothers me not knowing where he was all day. Of course, I refused to ask anyone about it. Then every night, my head would automatically turn toward the front when I would hear the door open, and I would kick myself.

Then tonight when I'm finally not thinking about him, he shows up looking so much better than he did in my head. His blue jeans hang on his hips with a brown belt, the black shirt tucked into the front with two buttons open at the collar. His arms are nice and bronzed, his eyes a light brown as he smiled at me. I couldn't help the smile that came out of me. "Hey, hey, hey." I hear Chelsea say and turn to look at her and Willow standing there. "Look at this place."

She smiles widely and throws her hands up in the air. I feel Asher's hand slide off my upper arm. The heat from his touch still lingers.

"Hey, Asher," Chelsea says. "Can I get something to drink?" I look over at him, and he just looks at me, then turns and smiles at Chelsea.

"Give me two beers and two shots of Jack," she says and then holds up her hand. "Three shots."

"I'm not doing a shot," I say, going to get the two beers while Asher gets the shots.

"Four, then," Willow says. "Asher can have one also."

"Thanks, ladies, but I don't drink on the job," he says with a smile. His charm just rolls off him, and I want to put my finger down my throat and fake gag. He pours the three shots and hands me one. "Cheers."

"To Amelia," Chelsea says, and I just glance at Asher as he gets someone a drink.

"To success," Willow says, holding up her shot.

I hold up my drink and clink it with the other two, taking the shot and wincing as the brown liquid burns all the way down to my stomach. "Yuck," I say and grab the two empty shot glasses and put them in the gray square container.

"We need new shot glasses." I look over at Reed, who is walking by with a tray of dirty glasses. On Saturday, Reed and his best friend Christopher bus tables, making sure we get clean glasses. They pick up and wipe down the tables.

"What do we have here?" Mayson says, coming to stand next to Chelsea. He pushes a guy who was standing too close to her away. I shake my head and roll my lips as the guy looks at him, and it takes one look from Mayson for the guy to move away. "Why are you drinking over here?"

"Well, because," Chelsea says, turning around and looking up at him. She's been in love with him since she was eighteen years old. Ethan invited him home. "We were doing a shot with Amelia."

"Can I get you guys something?" Asher says, coming to stand next to me.

"I'll have a beer," Mayson says, bringing Chelsea closer to him.

"I'll have one also," Quinn says. "And I'm not paying for it either."

"He's paying double," I tell Asher, who turns and just shakes his head.

"You work here?" Mayson looks at Asher.

"I thought for sure after the week you had, you'd be sitting in a tub of ice water," Quinn says, and I'm dying to ask him where he was all week.

"Hard work never killed anyone," Asher says and hands Quinn and Mayson two beers. Ethan comes over with Emily. "Besides, Ethan helped one day."

I want to ask them what everyone is talking about, but a song starts playing, and Chelsea throws her hands to the sky.

"This is our song." She claps her hands. "You"—she points at me—"get your skanky ass on that dance floor."

I laugh, shaking my head. "One"—I stick my finger up—"I'm not the one with a skanky ass." I turn to Mayson. "No offense."

"I don't even know what to say to that," Mayson says as we hear the sounds of the violin, and then I hear my name being called by the band I hired for the night.

"Where is Amelia?" He calls my name. Everyone looks over at me, and I put my head down.

"Go on," Asher says, standing beside me with his hand on my lower back. "I've got this covered, and if anything, Ethan can help me." I look over at Ethan, who shakes his head.

"No," he says. "I'm leaving."

Now Emily laughs. "Your two sisters are going on the dance floor." She claps her hands together. "There is no way in hell you are going to walk out of this bar." He glares at her, and she leans up and kisses the underside of his jaw. "And your wife." She turns. "Come on, Willow, let's dance."

Willow looks shocked when Emily grabs her hand and pulls her to the dance floor. I walk with them. "Okay," the singer says. "Where is she?"

"I'm here," I say, getting on the stage and looking out. "How is everyone doing tonight?" I ask the crowd, and they all cheer. "I have to say a huge thank-you to Gretchen for coming down and playing some tunes for us." I clap my hands and look at her as she nods at me.

"Now someone told me that this song right here is your song," Gretchen says, starting to play the tune again. "Who wants to see if Amelia still has her moves?" The crowd cheers, and I see my brother and my cousin Quinn both hang their heads as they push off the bar and make their way to the packed dance floor.

Asher just stands behind the bar as the dance floor makes a circle for us as I get down and stand in the middle of them . I see some of the girls standing beside the dance floor. The men stand beside them with their beer in their hands.

Quinn, Mayson, and Ethan stand there with their legs apart and their arms over their chest as they watch us. I clap my hands, looking over at Chelsea. "Your man is angry looking."

"He's all bark and no bite," she says, laughing as the music starts.

Willow stands at the end, talking to Emily, who just shrugs her shoulder. "Just follow those two."

When Gretchen starts singing, we do two steps to the front of the dance floor, and I see that Asher is there watching. His eyes are on me as I kick up one leg and dance backward to get to the middle. We clap our hands and start dancing to the left, then spinning to go back to the right. The crowd goes wild. We redo the steps over again, and this time, more people join us on the dance floor, even some of the men.

When it finally finishes, we get a round of applause, and I walk back to the bar. Asher is there, and he hands me a water bottle. "Thank you."

He doesn't say anything to me. He just nods his head, and he looks a little bit angry. "Cowboy," the blonde calls him over, and he claps his hands and walks over to them. He laughs and shakes his head as he puts one arm on the bar.

My family is back at the front of the bar when I walk to them. "What are we talking about?" Ethan says to the group, leaning on the bar.

"How Asher spent the whole week repairing your grandparents' fence around their property," Mayson says, and my head snaps to the side to look at Asher. As he pours six more shots for the women, my heart is beating so hard in my chest it's a wonder I can hear anything at this point.

"He worked his ass off fourteen, sometimes fifteen hours a day," Ethan says, shaking his head.

"He had no choice. If he didn't show up early enough, Billy was out there with his tractor," Mayson says, shaking his head. "He even called me a pussy when I showed up at six a.m."

"That is where he went this whole week?" I mumble under my breath.

Asher comes back over and looks at us. "What's wrong?" he asks, looking at me.

"You built a fence with my grandfather?" I ask, and

he just shrugs.

"He needed help," Asher says. "I had time to spare."

"Why are you lying?" Quinn says, shaking his head.

"I'm not lying," he says, pushing away from the bar and walking over to the other side of the bar.

"He worked one day from three a.m., took a break for breakfast, and then worked until nine at night," Quinn says. "And still did his rounds to all the farms."

"Well, he did get a fucking great tan," Mayson says, leaning on the bar.

I don't say anything because all I can do is look at him as he serves a couple of women and smiles at them politely. They both check him out when he walks away from them and then look at each other and share a giggle. He comes back over to us, and he has no idea what he does to these women.

"Can we get some more shots over here?" the girls ask Asher, and I know I have to get away for a bit and clear my head.

"I'm going to make my rounds and make sure everything is okay," I tell Chelsea, and she nods. I walk out of the bar, and I catch Asher watching me as I head over to the sports bar. I open the door and see that people are starting to leave as the game just finished.

"Is everything okay?" Reed says from beside me with a gray bin in his hand. He stands six foot two, wearing blue jeans and a black shirt. He's filled out in the last couple of years.

"How is the ice situation?" I ask.

"Half full," he says. "I'm about to take out the trash."

"I got it," I say. "Finish cleaning the tables in the sports room so she can close up as soon as the rest of the people leave."

"Don't pick up anything heavy," Reed tells me, and I laugh at him.

"I could probably bench-press you," I say, and he laughs.

"Yeah, you and Chelsea together," he says, and I just shake my head. I walk around the bar, picking up some trash on my way to the back.

I tie one of the big black bags and lift it out of the bin. I walk over to the back door, pushing it open with my ass as I walk out into the cool air. The two spotlights in the back are out, and I look up, shaking my head. "Fuck," I say as I walk over to the dumpster all the way at the end of the property. My head is down while I walk, and when I look up, all I feel is a burning sensation to my head, and everything goes black.

Thirteen

Asher

"DO YOU WANT another beer?" I ask Ethan while I wipe down the bar in front of him. He shakes his head. I walk down the bar, ignoring the need to look up and find Amelia. The bar is slowly starting to get less crowded, and I look up and see that it's almost one o'clock. The band finished their last song thirty minutes ago, and it's just a playlist that plays. The dance floor is still semi full.

"Can we have more shots, Cowboy?" the group of girls yells from the other end of the bar, and I look at the ceiling and count to ten. I turn to walk toward them when Reed comes behind the bar to grab the dirty glasses.

"Shots, shots, shots," one of the girls says, laughing at herself, putting her hands in the air and dancing.

"If they vomit," Reed says, grabbing the bin, then

looking at me, "I'm not cleaning it."

"That is what you are paid to do, little brother," Quinn tells him, and he glares at him. "Hey, you think we never cleaned up vomit?"

"Not me," Chelsea says, grabbing her bottle of beer and taking a pull of it. "I was the one doing the vomiting most of the time." I laugh, and Mayson shakes his head, and she looks over at him. "Better or worse." She leans into him, and he kisses her lips.

Reed looks at me and then the girls. "Ladies." They all look at him. "Why don't you go dance, and I'll fill up the shot glasses, on the house?" he says, giving them a smile.

"Really?" the blonde says, and I look over at Ethan, who just shares a look with me.

"You betcha," he says. "Six shots will be waiting here for you guys, on the house." He winks at them, and they giggle and take off to the dance floor.

Reed turns to me with a smug look on his face. "Now you can fill up six shot glasses with water," Reed says. "They won't even notice."

He grabs the bin and walks out of the bar area toward the back. "I bet you twenty bucks they notice," Willow says, looking at Quinn. I grab the six shot glasses and fill them with water as the rest place bets and then leave them in front of their seats.

"Here they come," Willow says, and the six of them just sit at the bar watching the girls as

they come back, swinging their hips, stumbling, and laughing. They each grab a glass and raise it up. "To the cool cowboy," one of them says, and they take the shot.

"Smooth," one of them says.

"I've had this before," another one says while she looks into the empty glass.

One of them looks up at me. "What was in this? It was good."

I try not to laugh at them. "It was a secret drink only he knows," I tell them, and they turn around, going back to the dance floor.

"You owe me twenty bucks," Quinn says to Willow, "but I can be persuaded to take other forms of payment."

"You're gross," Chelsea says. "We are right here." Ethan laughs at them bickering.

"Where is Amelia?" I finally say, looking around the bar and not spotting her.

"Probably in the bathroom," Chelsea says.

I look over the heads of people, trying to spot her. The crowd has thinned out even more than before. "I'm going to check around," I tell Ethan, and he nods, coming behind the bar. I walk toward the sports room and open it to see it's almost empty.

"Hey, Dolly," I call her name, and she looks up from cleaning the bar. "Have you seen Amelia?"

"No." She shakes her head. "I've been slammed all night, so I haven't seen anything." I nod at her and turn to walk out of the room, going to the pool table area and seeing that only one game is going on and there are six people there.

"Hey," Christopher says, looking at me while he walks around the area, picking up all the empty beer bottles that have been left. "What's up?"

"Have you seen Amelia?" I ask, looking around toward the bar to see if she got back.

"Not in a while," he answers, placing the bottles in the bin with the sound of clinking.

"If you see her, tell her I'm looking for her." I walk toward the dance floor, looking through the crowd. Maybe she got sucked onto the dance floor, and I didn't see her. The burning in my stomach starts, and my heart beats faster as the time goes on and I still can't find her.

Making my way past where the band is loading up their stuff, I look in the back room but don't see anyone there. I even go to the office. The soft light on the desk is on, but it's empty.

Making my way back to the bar, Ethan looks up at me while he wipes down the bar. "Did you find her?"

"No," I say, shaking my head.

"I'll go and check the bathroom," Chelsea says, pushing off from the bar and walking to the back.

I spot Reed coming back and picking up the empty beer bottles left on the tables. "Reed!" I shout his name, and he walks over to us. "Have you seen Amelia?"

"Yeah, she was going out back to take out the trash," he says, and I look over at Ethan, who has stopped cleaning at this point.

Mayson stands up and so does Quinn. "She isn't back there," Chelsea says, and the four of us all move at the same pace.

I push out of the door first, and I'm shocked at how dark it is. "Where are the lights?" Ethan asks, and we look up to see the two spotlights are out.

"They were working last week. I checked them when I changed the ones in the front," I say.

The sound of truck doors close in the distance as people are leaving. "I'm going to go and check the garbage," Ethan says. "You go and check to see if she is in the front. Maybe she's talking to someone."

I nod at him as I turn to walk toward the end of the building, jogging a bit, and all I see when I turn the corner of the building is people walking to their cars. The sound of rocks crunching and women laughing fill the air.

"I found her!" Ethan yells, and I can tell from the sound of his voice that something is wrong. "Call nine-one-one." Quinn has his phone out already.

My breathing starts to come in pants as I run back to Ethan as he squats next to her. She lies there not moving with the garbage bag beside her. "I need light!" I shout, my hands shaking as I look at her lying there in the dark. The fact that I don't know what is wrong with her makes my whole body go cold. "Mayson!" I yell his name, and he comes over. "Block off this whole area," I start to tell him. "No one comes here except the ambulance." I look back down at Amelia, scared to touch her in case she is cold. "Quinn," I call his name, and he looks at me. "Make sure no one leaves the fucking bar until we get statements from everyone." I grab my phone out of my pocket and open the flashlight. "Did you check to see if she's …?"

"I checked her pulse," Ethan says, and Chelsea comes running out.

"What happened to her?" she asks frantically. "Don't move her." She grabs my phone out of my hands, and I feel helpless, but I know Chelsea can help. She moves the phone to her head. "No blood," she says with a sigh of relief. "That's a good thing." My hand comes out to grab hers, and I feel the heat.

"Did she fall?" I ask, looking around. The sound of rocks crunching comes closer and closer.

"Guess my dad is here," Ethan says. I hear two doors shut, and I know he didn't come by himself.

"Amelia," Jacob says, followed by Kallie. "What happened?" Ethan moves over as Kallie comes to squat next to him. Her hand comes out to grab Amelia.

"We don't know," I answer before Ethan. "We found her out here. She was lying there unconscious." I'm about to continue talking when we hear Amelia groan.

Everyone stops talking and moving as we look at her. She moves her head side to side, and her eyes slowly flutter open. Kallie sobs out in relief, and all I can do is squeeze her hand tighter. "Hey," Chelsea says, leaning in to look at Amelia. Amelia moans out and tries to sit up, but Chelsea puts her hand on her shoulder. "Don't move until the medics get here."

"They are three minutes out," Jacob says, and Amelia turns her head to look at her father.

"What are you doing here?" she asks him.

"Someone get her water!" I shout, and Willow nods her head at me and turns to run back into the bar. "What do you remember?" I ask, and she looks at me. What feels like an electric shock runs through me.

"I was coming out to bring the garbage," she says. "Then I felt burning in my head." She moves. "I want to sit up."

"You shouldn't move until the medics get here," Chelsea says, but Amelia, with her stubbornness, ignores her and sits up.

She slips her hand out of mine as she touches the back of her head. She winces. "There is a bump."

"Were you outside by yourself?" I ask, and she looks at me. "I don't really know." She shakes her head, and the sound of the ambulance comes closer and closer.

"Isn't it too dark to assess her here?" I look at Jacob. "Maybe we can get a couple of the cars moved and turn on our headlights."

"I'll go and move mine," Quinn says.

Willow comes running out with a cold water bottle in her hand. "Here," she says, handing me the bottle.

"Can you move my truck to the side and aim the headlights this way?" I ask her, and she nods her head. Emily runs with her to move their car also. Chelsea gets up, making room for the medics coming with bags in their hands.

"Sorry," one of the medics says, and I get up, giving him room. I walk over to stand next to Jacob, the lights from the cars giving us some light.

"What do we have here?" the medic asks Amelia.

"I don't know," Amelia answers honestly. Her voice is soft. "I was taking out the garbage, and the next thing you know, I'm waking up with everyone around me."

"Did you fall?" he asks, taking out gloves to put on.

"I don't think so." She shakes her head. "I don't …" She closes her eyes, and I rush to her as she almost falls back.

"I got you," I say softly to her.

"Maybe you lost your footing?" Kallie says, and I look to see that Jacob has her in his arms.

"I felt," she says, "something behind me." My blood runs cold as ice. "When I went to turn around, that is when I felt the burning, and everything went black."

Fourteen

AMELIA

I FEEL THE heat from his chest on my back as he sits behind me and holds me up. My head's still spinning, and when I close my eyes, my stomach lurches like a wave in the pool. "What do you mean you felt something? Was it something or someone?" Asher asks, and I can tell he's angry from his tone.

"I don't know," I answer honestly. "I walked out, I was looking down, and then I felt as if I was being followed."

"Are the cameras up yet?" Asher asks, and I look over to see who he is asking.

"They are up," my father says and gets his phone out. "I'm going to call Casey."

"Wait a second." I hold up my hand. "Who put

cameras up?"

"Your father," my mother says. "And I, for one, am not going to say I told you so." She looks over at him. "But I'm happy he did."

"We are going to have words," I tell my father but stop talking when the medic takes my blood pressure. "When my head isn't spinning."

"I can't wait," he says, and I close my eyes and lean back against Asher for a minute while I try to get my head to stop spinning.

"Her blood pressure is a little high," the medic says. "But that's normal."

"Shouldn't she be assessed by a doctor?" Asher asks from behind me.

"She's going," my father says, "even if I have to carry her."

"We can get the stretcher," the medic says, "but with the rocks …"

"I'll carry her," Asher says from behind me, and before I even know what's going on, I'm in his arms. One arm under my knees and the other around my back. "I've got you," he says, and I look up at his chest as he carries me all the way to the waiting ambulance. He steps into the back without skipping a beat.

He places me in the middle of the stretcher. "I have to stay here and make sure we get everyone's statement," he says, and all I can do is nod my head. I don't trust myself not to ask him to come with me. I don't trust myself around him. He makes me want things that I vowed never to yearn for.

"I'm going to go with her," my mother says from beside Asher. "I'll keep you all informed."

"Thank you," Asher says, taking one last look at me and then getting out of the ambulance. One of the medics steps into the back and closes the door. I put my head back, and a tear escapes.

"It's going to be okay, baby girl," my mother says, grabbing my hand in hers. "Before you know it, you'll be home, and this will all be over."

"I'm fine, Mom," I say.

"Always so strong," she says, and I see her wipe her own eyes. "It's okay to need help, Amelia." I don't answer her. Instead, I close my eyes.

When we get to the hospital, they pull me out, and I don't know why I'm shocked that Chelsea is waiting for us. "You don't have to be here," I say, shaking my head. "I'm fine."

"Um …" She looks at me and then down. "I was given strict orders to come here and not leave your side."

"Can my father exaggerate any more?" I chuckle, and so does my mother.

"It wasn't your father," she says. My head whips back to look at her, and it's the wrong move to do because it makes my stomach rise, and I lean over the side and vomit.

"Oh, my," my mother says, putting her hand to her mouth.

"I'm not a doctor," Chelsea says, "but I think she has a concussion."

"Here, rinse your mouth." My mother runs to me with

a bottle of water.

I grab the bottle, not even giving a shit that I just threw up in the middle of the parking lot, and rinse my mouth out. "Ready?" they ask me, and I nod my head.

We get into the room, and I look up at Chelsea, who is typing away on her phone. "I'm not going to put in this text that you threw up," she says, "because no one needs to know that."

"This whole thing is ridiculous," I finally say. "I fell and hit my head."

"Well, as soon as the doctor tells us that, we can go." My mother folds her arms over her chest, and I know that no matter what I say, she isn't going to let me leave here until the doctor sees me.

I don't have to wait long. He comes in, and after thirty minutes, he sends me for tests and finally comes back and tells me that I have a concussion. "Do you have anyone at home who can monitor you for the next twenty-four hours?" the doctor asks me.

"I can do it," Chelsea tells him. "I work with Dr. Gabe."

"Perfect," the doctor says. "Now on to the nitty-gritty stuff.

"No work for the next five days at least." My mouth opens, and I'm about to argue with him when he says, "You're lucky it isn't seven."

"But ..." I say.

"Your brain just suffered a contusion," he says. "Which means you have to give it rest to get back to normal."

"We will make sure she rests," my mother says, and I turn to glare at her, but she ignores me.

"Limit the time you watch television or you're on the computer," he says. "The minute you get a headache, you have to start back at day one."

"After five days, I can go to work?" I ask.

"For a couple of hours," he says. "But you have to be headache-free for five days before you even go back to work." He smiles at me. "You're lucky that your head didn't crack open."

"Oh, yeah," I say sarcastically. "So lucky."

He laughs and walks out of the room. "Let's get you home," my mother says.

I stand and walk out with both of them at my side. "Are you hungry?" Chelsea asks, and I shake my head. I get into the back seat of the truck, and my mother gets in next to me.

"The guys are still at the bar," Chelsea says, and I look at them. "It's been three hours?"

I look out the window now as Chelsea drives toward my mother's house. Pulling up, I see that the lights are on outside.

My mother opens the door and then comes to open the door in the back, sticking her head inside. "Are you sure you don't want me to stay with you?" she asks, her hand going to my cheek.

"No, I'll be okay, and if I need you, I'll call you," I say, and she leans over and kisses my cheek.

"I'll come by in the morning to bring you food," she tells me, "and you promise to call me if you need me."

She looks at me now, waiting for me to answer her and mean it.

"I promise," I say, and I hug her before she gets out of the truck and closes the door. I close my eyes as we make the four-minute drive to my house, and when we pull up, I am suddenly disappointed that Asher is not here. I push it far down when I get out of the truck, and I walk up the step and into the house.

"Go take a shower," Chelsea tells me. "Just don't close the door."

I walk toward my bedroom and stop and turn around. "Who told you to come to the hospital?" I ask.

She avoids my eyes and puts her purse on the couch, and then goes to sit down. "Are you sure you want to know?"

"If I asked you, it's because I want to know," I say, ignoring the heat that comes up my neck.

"Asher," she says his name, and I close my eyes. "He was a mess," she says and I hold up my hand.

"I'm sure he would have been that way for any of us." I turn, not ready to have this conversation with her. Not ready to have this conversation with anyone actually. Making my way to the shower, I stand under the hot water for a couple of minutes, letting it seep into me.

When I woke up in the dark, I was so confused and scared. Especially when I couldn't remember where I was. Then I heard his voice and felt his hand in mine, and a calmness came over me. I knew I would be okay.

When I walk back out of the bathroom, Chelsea is sitting on my bed with her phone in her hand. "How do you feel?"

"Tired," I say, climbing into bed. "And like I got hit on the head with a baseball bat."

"I think that is pretty accurate," Chelsea says, laughing from beside me.

"On a scale of one to ten …" I look over at her. "Do you think anyone is going to forget that I can't go to work on Monday?"

She gets up and laughs, shaking her head. "I'm going to go with one hundred."

I laugh at her, knowing the last thing anyone in my family will let me forget is that I have to be rested. I'm about to say something when we both hear the front door open and slam closed.

I hear the boots on the floor, and I hold my breath, hoping that he just goes to his room. But I should have known better than that. His body fills the doorway, and my heart speeds up while my mouth gets suddenly dry.

"Asher," I say his name in almost a whisper. He looks like he's been through war. His hands are dirty, and his face shows that he has dirt also on his cheek.

"Hey," he says, walking into the room. "I got here as soon as I could. How are you feeling?"

"I'm okay," I answer him, and his eyes never leave mine.

"Mayson is waiting for you outside." He finally turns to Chelsea.

"I thought you were going to stay with me." I look over at Chelsea. "You told the doctor that you would watch me." I sit up, ignoring the way my head throbs.

"I told her that I would do it," Asher says, and Chelsea just looks at me, trying to hide her smile. "It made no sense for her to stay here with you." I want to tell him it makes no sense for him to stay here with me, but all the words get stuck in my throat. "I can look after her," Asher says, and Chelsea just shrugs.

"I'll call you later," she says, leaning over and hugging me. "Go easy on him," she whispers in my ear, and she kisses my cheek.

"Thank you," he tells her when she gets close to him, "for keeping me in the loop tonight."

"I didn't think I had much choice in that matter," she tells him and then turns to me. "Call me as soon as you wake up tomorrow." I just nod at her as she looks back at Asher one last time and then walks out of the house.

"Do you need anything?" Asher asks me, and I can see that his shirt is dirty and so are his jeans, and I wonder what he has been up to.

"No," I say. "I'm fine." He just stands there with his hands on his hips, looking at me. "I don't need anyone to look after me."

"Why are you like this?" he asks, throwing up his hands. "Why can't you just accept the help?" He runs his hands through his hair. His brown eyes looking almost black.

"Because I learned a long time ago that I can only depend on myself." I wipe away the tear before it falls down my cheek. "I learned that the hard way." I swallow down the lump that was building up. "And I'll never go through that again."

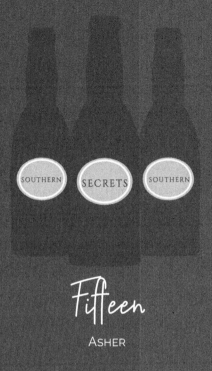

Fifteen

Asher

SHE LOOKS STRAIGHT in my eyes, her voice never wavering as she says the words that I know hurt her. "And I'll never go through that again."

I want to ask her all the questions, but I know there is a time and place for that, and it's not that time. I also know that if she gives me her truth, I have to give her mine. "I have to take a shower," I say, looking down at myself. "Are you going to be okay for ten minutes?"

"I'm going to bed," she says, sinking into her bed. "Can you turn off the lights out there?" she asks, and all I can do is nod at her. Even if I wanted to tell her no, the lump in my throat at seeing that she is okay stops me. I didn't know what I would be walking in on. The last time I saw her, she looked scared.

"Chelsea said I have to wake you up every two hours," I say, and she rolls her eyes. I watch her turn on her side in a fetal position and bring the covers under her chin. "Good night, Amelia," I say softly, turning and walking out of the room.

My whole body on alert, I walk to the front door and lock up. Turning off the lights, I walk to the back door and make sure that it's locked also. I walk to the bathroom, taking off the dusty clothes and dumping them in the corner. Getting into the shower, I hang my head as the hot water washes over me.

Leaving her in that ambulance and not going with her shifted something inside me, and I knew then and there that whatever this shit was had to stop. I worked side by side with Jacob the whole time. My only focus was finding out what happened to her.

The phone in my back pocket felt heavier and heavier with each message. My ability not to want to kill someone slipped away, each time. Jacob had to send me away from a couple of the guys we were interviewing because if one of them said again that she was smoking hot, I was going to throat punch them.

I get out of the shower and slip on a pair of boxers and shorts. I walk back to her bedroom and see she's still sleeping. I think about walking to her bed and lying down beside her just so I can make sure she is okay all night long. My heart pushes me to go, but my head, my head moves my feet away from her door, and I walk over to the couch to lie down and set my phone alarm to go off in two hours. I turn on my back and look up at the ceiling, my eyes never closing to sleep when I hear the soft alarm. I get up and walk to the bedroom. Her eyes open slowly when I walk in. "Did you set an alarm?" she asks me softly.

"Yeah," I tell her and see that the sun is coming up. "Go back to sleep."

"Turn off your alarm," she grumbles out, "or I'll break the phone."

I laugh. "How is your head?"

"It's not my head that hurts. It's the pain in my ass in front of me that's bothering me." She turns in her bed. "Now, let me sleep."

"Call me if you need anything," I say, and I want to just sit and make sure she is okay, but instead, I walk back to the couch, and this time, sleep comes and takes me. The sound of movement makes my eyes fly open, and I see that the sun is streaming into the room. "Hey," I say, getting up seeing her in the kitchen.

"Why are you sleeping on the couch?" She looks over at me, and she looks tired but still so beautiful that she takes my breath away.

"I was scared I wouldn't hear you," I say, getting up as she walks to the cupboard and gets two mugs out. She wears another pair of shorts and a long-sleeve sweater. "How are you feeling?"

"Annoyed," she says, pouring coffee in the mugs and then putting the pot back. "I got seventeen voice messages from my grandmother." She hands me a cup of coffee. "One text from my grandfather." She goes back to her mug and smells it right before she drinks it. "A text from every single cousin and my mother should be here any minute."

I walk to the fridge, grabbing some milk and putting a splash in my coffee. "Are you hungry?"

"My mother is coming, and I'm assuming from the voice mails from my grandmother, she has cooked everything that I've ever said I liked since I was a little girl," she says, and I smile.

"Nothing wrong with family loving you," I say, taking another sip, and I see her face soften just a bit.

"I didn't mean," she says softly.

I shake my head. "You don't have to apologize." It looks like she is going to say something else, but the front door opens.

"Incoming," Amelia says to me, holding her coffee cup in both hands.

"Good morning." I look over my shoulder and see Kallie standing there with her hands full of food. "Oh, good, you had coffee." I laugh and then look down when Amelia glares at me. "Good morning, Asher," Kallie says.

I walk over to her to help grab some things from her hands. "Here, let me help you there, Mrs. McIntyre."

"Suck-up," Amelia grumbles when I walk back with all the food in my hands. Placing the food on the island, Kallie walks over to Amelia and holds her face in her hands. "I'm fine."

"When aren't you fine?" she asks her daughter and then turns around. "What do you want to eat?" she asks, grabbing plates out of the cupboard.

"If you guys are going to be okay," I say to them, "I'm going to go and meet up with the guys." I look at them, and Amelia just stares at me.

"You can do whatever you want," she says, her eyes going down to the food in front of her. I look over at Kallie, who smiles at me, and I see tears in her eyes. "I'll be fine."

"Oh, we know," I say, turning and walking back to the bedroom. I slip on a pair of jeans and a T-shirt. When I walk back out, Kallie is the only one there. "Where is she?"

"She went to lie down," Kallie says softly.

"I won't be long," I say, and she looks down at her hands and then looks up again.

"Asher," she says my name, and I look over to where Amelia's bedroom is. "She isn't good with people helping her."

"Yeah, I got that pretty loud and clear," I say and she smiles and a lone tear escapes.

"She's worth it," she says and then walks toward Amelia's room. I want to tell her that I know she's worth it. I want to tell her that I'm the one who isn't worth it. All the support that this family has given me and I'm not worthy of any of it.

I grab my keys and walk out to the truck, the phone ringing in my hand. I see it's Ethan. "Morning," I say, getting into the truck and starting it.

"We are at the clubhouse," he says.

"Be there in ten," I say and disconnect. When I get there, I see more cars than are usually there. I walk in, and the door is buzzed open right away. I look around and see that some of the guys are here.

Ethan sits at a desk with a cup of coffee in his hand, leaning back in the chair. Jacob stands with Casey beside him. "Morning," I say, walking toward them.

"Just in time," Casey says to me. "We were just going over the camera feed."

I sit on one of the desks while the screens fill with the back of the bar. "Nothing is out of sorts," Casey says, and then I see the door open and the light comes out from inside, showing Amelia walking out carrying the garbage bag.

She walks with her head down but something in the corner makes me sit up. "Stop it," I snap out. "Go back a couple of seconds and look at the side corner." I point and Casey goes back and starts it again. You see a dark figure, but if you weren't looking for it, you wouldn't have seen it. What caught my eye was the orange dot. "That's a cigarette," I say and we all watch as the man steps out of his corner, flicking his cigarette. He moves behind her and lifts his hand, hitting her over the head. My hands go into fists when I see her fall. The figure stands over her, not moving. He turns and just walks away from her, his head down with a hoodie blocking his face. "We can't see anything." I shake my head. "But." I look up. "He left his DNA."

"I'm going to go out there and see if I can find it," Ethan says.

"He wasn't there for ten minutes," I say. "He was camping out there, so chances are there are more than a couple to choose from."

I look back at Jacob, who shares a look with Casey as Ethan walks out of the room. "You were right," Casey says, shaking his head. "You lost me a thousand dollars." He walks over to me and slaps my shoulder. "Glad I lost this one."

"What are you talking about?" I ask, and he smiles. "I'll let Jacob talk to you. I'm going to go and help my father."

I watch Casey walk out of the room and then turn to Jacob. "What am I missing?"

He stands there tapping his finger on the middle of table. "Have you ever thought about what you want to do in life?" I just look at him.

"To be honest, I don't even know if I'm staying," I say, admitting it finally, and he just looks at me. "My whole life I went from place to place. I figured if I was supposed to be in one place, the universe would let me know." I fold my arms over my chest. "The fire burning everything I have was a sign I should be moving along."

"Or it could be a sign that you were wasting away at working on a farm when you should be following what you're good at."

"And what is that?" I ask.

"Seeing you at the fire and then again last night. And here this morning proves to me what I've thought all along. You were made for this," he says. "Let's just look at what we just saw. Hell, I didn't even see the guy in the corner."

"That doesn't mean anything," I say. "I'm observant."

"You are more than that. You have good instincts," he says. "You had the scene of the crime closed off even before I got there last night. You are protective, you have problem-solving skills, and you have the heart for it. That's not something that you learn. That's something instilled in you."

"I never had anyone in my whole life care about what I did," I say, and I know I should stop. "Never had a father figure guide me toward the right path. Never had anyone give a shit at what I was good at. It's a lot to take in and think about."

He comes to me. "That's all I can ask you," he says. "It's time to set some roots. Maybe you were led here for a reason." He slaps my shoulder. "I want you to think about it, and I want you to know that I'm here for you regardless of what you decide. You're one of the good ones, Asher."

He walks out and leaves me alone, my eyes looking up at the black screen. "Would he ask you to stay if he knew the truth?" I ask myself.

Sixteen

AMELIA

"WHAT THE FUCK are you doing here?" I hear growled and look up to see Quinn standing in my office at the barn.

"It's been three days. I'm fine," I say, and he shakes his head. "And I'm bored," I admit. "The last three days have been going at a snail's pace. I can't watch television; I can't get on my phone. I can't go to the bar because my father has guys stationed outside, and people are constantly hovering all over me." I throw my hands up in frustration.

"Who are these people?" He leans against the door, crossing his arms and his legs. He tries to hide the smile fighting to come out.

"Well, for one, Mother." I put my finger up. "She is

there every single morning to make sure I wake up okay."

"That's her job," he reminds me, making me glare at him.

"Then there is Asher." I put my second finger up, and I can see his eyes are going just a touch lighter as he listens to me. "Guy sleeps on the couch every night, and he wakes me up every fucking two hours."

"He's making sure you are okay." He shrugs.

"I'm fine!" I shout out. "I don't have headaches. I don't have dizziness. I'm fine. One hundred percent fine."

"Hey, what are you doing here?" I look over and see Ethan standing there.

"This is where I work," I say. "That is my name on the door." I point at the door I added my name to last year when I got into a fight with Quinn.

Ethan looks at Quinn. "I know you work here, smart-ass. What I'm asking is why are you here? Chelsea said you have to be off work for seven days."

"Five days," I say, holding up my hand. "Not seven."

"Well, I don't know about you," Ethan says. "But Sunday." He sticks out his thumb. "Monday." His other finger comes out. "Tuesday."

I hold up my hand. "I get it. You know how to count and the days of the week." I glare at him.

"Come on," he says to me. "Let's go for a ride."

"I have a ton of work to do here," I say, looking at my desk and seeing that there is actually nothing for me to do. "Who did my work?"

"Willow," Quinn says. "She was worried you would

be a basket case when you came back."

"I don't know why everyone thinks I'm grouchy." I get up and walk to them. "I'm perfectly happy." I force the smile. "And chipper."

"You look like the Joker in *Batman,*" Quinn says, and I punch his arm. "I'm telling your mom on you."

I'm about to punch him again when Ethan pulls my arm out of the office. "Come on," he says, pulling me out of the barn. "Let's go visit Grandpa and get your horse."

"Ugh, fine," I say, getting in the truck with him. "You're annoying, by the way."

"That's my job as an older brother," he says, smirking. "Literally my only job."

"Really?" I look over at him. "I thought Dad said it was to protect me."

"And bother you," he adds in. "You know, to make up for all the times you woke me up in the middle of the night."

"I was a child," I say, shaking my head as we get to the barn. I get out laughing. "I had no way of knowing it was wrong."

"What about when you came into my room when you were seven and painted my nails when I was sleeping?"

I roll my eyes when I look up and see my grandfather coming to us. His face fills with a smile, and I can't help the smile that comes on my face. "There she is." His voice is soft, and I walk to him, hugging him.

"Hi, Grandpa," I say, smiling up at him. His big white cowboy hat is on his head.

"What are you doing out of bed?" he asks me. I roll my eyes, and he shakes his head, laughing. "Just like her momma."

"We are going to go for a ride," Ethan says. "I'm not saddling your horse," he says as we walk to the barn with my grandfather's arm around my shoulder.

"Don't touch my horse," I tell Ethan, and we walk into the barn as I walk to my stall and saddle my horse.

"Be careful with her," my grandfather tells Ethan. "If she gets hurt, I'll tan your hide."

"Grandpa, I'm almost thirty." He laughs at him, and my grandfather stands there with his hands on his hips. "Fine, I'll make sure she is okay."

We ride side by side, the sun high in the sky as we go into the forest. "Don't you work?" I ask Ethan, and he laughs.

"I am working," he says, looking at me.

"Am I your work?" I shriek. "You guys are all assholes."

He laughs. "We just want to make sure you're okay."

"Yeah, well, still," I say as we ride slowly through the woods, neither of us saying anything. Both of us are lost in our own thoughts.

"So what's the deal with you and Asher?" I look over at him.

"There is no deal with Asher and me. His place burned down, and I offered him a place to sleep."

"I did," Ethan says, not looking at me. "We all did. But he didn't take anyone else up on their offer."

I shrug, not wanting to think about it anymore. "I

guess you have to ask him why he said yes to me and not to you."

Ethan must sense my mood because the rest of the ride is quiet, and when we finally get back to the barn and leave the horses, he says, "Mom wants us to have dinner at her house."

"Oh, that sounds good," I say because for the past three days, I've been sitting on the couch trying not to think about why Asher was coming home later than usual. The only answer that I had was that he was seeing someone. The thought made me fucking sick to my stomach, and I hate that it makes me feel this way. I wish I felt nothing.

We pull up to my parents' house, and I see Emily out with Gabriel and Aubrey on her hip. "Daddy," Gabriel says, jumping up and down while Aubrey claps her hands together. I look over and see that Ethan's whole face lights up. He gets out of the truck and walks to them, and I watch for a second as I wait for the sadness to pass. It's what I thought I would have. I wait for the moment to pass like it always does before I get out.

"Look who is here," Ethan says, and Gabriel runs over to me, smashing his face into my chest.

"Auntie Amelia," he says, looking up at me. I kiss his head and scrunch my nose at him, something I used to do to him ever since he was young. "Daddy said you fell and hit your head."

"I did," I say, walking into the house.

"You should wear a helmet," he says, and I laugh at him. I walk into our childhood home, the smell of cooking filling the air.

"Momma," I say when I get inside and make my way to the kitchen. Her eyes light up when she sees me.

"Look at you," she says. "You have color in your cheeks."

"I did that," Ethan says, coming in and going straight to the fridge.

"Did you wash your hands?" my mother asks him, and he rolls his eyes.

"He did not," I tell my mother as I walk to the sink and start to wash my hands.

"Tattletale," Ethan mumbles under his breath as he comes up and pushes me over, making me laugh.

"What is all this noise?" I hear my father say, coming in the side door. I turn my head, smiling, and then I see Asher behind him.

"Now this is what I like to see," my father says. "The family all under one roof." My heart speeds up, and my stomach sinks when Asher looks at me and then turns his eyes right away to my mother as she talks to him. I dry my hands on the towel and avoid looking at him.

"What can I do to help?" I ask my mother quietly as Ethan, Asher, and my father stand in the kitchen looking around.

"You can wash the salad," my mother says, and I bend my head, going over to the sink and grabbing the bowl to place the salad in.

The noise around me goes up just a notch, but I keep my head down, trying not to think about where he is. My mother works around me, and Emily also comes in to help. I feel so out of sorts, and it's crazy.

"Mom, is there any ginger ale?" I ask, and she nods her head.

"In the garage fridge." I nod at her and walk toward the garage. Opening the door and walking down the four steps, I'm about to pull open the fridge when I feel eyes on me.

I turn my head, seeing Asher there leaning against my mother's parked car with his phone in his hand. "Hey," he says when I look at him.

"Hi," I mumble and then turn to grab my drink and get out of there. My stomach feels like it's spinning around and around.

"Are you okay?" Asher asks, pushing himself off the car and walking over to me.

"I'm fine, why?" I avoid looking at him as I duck my head. I feel him right beside me. His hand comes up, going under my chin. He lifts my head, and my eyes meet his. "What?" I ask, the sounds of my heart beating echoing so loud in my ears I can't even hear myself talk.

"Ever since I walked into the house, you've become quiet," he says, his voice soft, and he steps in even closer as his hand falls from under my chin.

"I was just surprised to see you here," I answer honestly.

"Yeah, and why is that?" His voice goes low as he steps up even closer to me, and I feel the fridge against my back.

"I don't know," I answer, frustrated. "You're fucking everywhere I turn."

"And that bothers you?" His eyes go a deep brown

to where they look almost black. "Why?" he whispers. He is so close I can feel his breath on me. His hand comes up as he takes a piece of my hair in his fingers. My whole body is on high alert, and my body braces itself. "Why does me being here bother you, Amelia?" He says my name, and I lick my lips as I feel his head get even close to me. I want to put my hands on his hips. I want to tilt my head back just a touch more and ask him for the kiss I've been dying for. "I've gotten under your skin," he says, and I want to tell him that he's wrong. I want to tell him that he hasn't gotten under anything. "Good," he says, and his head moves in close. "Because you've gotten under mine," he says, and I feel like I'm in a trance. The whole world could be crumbling around me, and I wouldn't think twice. I also wouldn't care. The only thing that I want is for him to kiss me.

"Asher," I say his name in a whisper, or a plea, even I don't know anymore.

"What, baby?" he says, and my heart surges to my throat, and my hands are finally moving to his chest. His heart beats under my hand as much as mine is beating. I tilt my head to the side, and I can taste his lips on mine.

"Auntie Amelia!" Gabriel yells, and we both jump apart, the both of us panting. "Grandma wants you."

I look at Asher, who stands there, his eyes never leaving me. "Coming," I say, turning and walking away from him.

Seventeen

Asher

I STARE INTO the eyes of the woman who has haunted my dreams and thoughts for the last I don't even know. But nothing can compare to looking into the real thing. Her eyes are a soft blue, a crystal blue that you can see right through her.

I can feel her heart beating just as fast as mine, as her chest rises and falls. The heat of her hands that were on my chest, like she branded me with her touch. "Coming," Amelia says and slips out from in front of me. She walks back up the stairs without a second glance back at me and goes into the house. The door slams shut, making me aware that what just happened now was a mistake. The guilt settles in my stomach as I think about how much over the line I just crossed.

I hang my head as my chest rises up and down as if I just chased off a wild pack of wolves. I can't move from my spot, the smell of lavender still all around me. My body knows she was right here and refuses to move.

"What the fuck was I thinking?" I ask myself as I put my head back and look at the ceiling of the garage. "What the hell was I doing?" I shake my head. "In her parents' house. With her brother and her father mere steps away from us." I wasn't; that was the point of it. When I walked into the house and saw her laughing and smiling, it just … The answer was so blatant and so easy. Bottom line, I couldn't fucking help myself.

Following Jacob into his house, the last thing I was surprised to see was her in the kitchen laughing. I had to get away from her as fast as I could, so I ducked out and came out to the garage. Trying to convince myself that whatever I was thinking about and whatever I was feeling was the worst idea I've ever had in my whole life. And I've had some stupid ideas that got me into hot water more than once, but this, with her, I'd be cut off at the knees.

I just couldn't control myself with her standing there in front of me. Her eyes were changing right before my eyes. Pissed because I was everywhere she turned. Happy knowing that I got under her skin just as much. The information broke the little strength I had left in me. My head was yelling at me that it was the stupidest thing I've ever done in my life, yet my heart, my heart was telling me that this moment is what I've been waiting for my whole life.

The past three days have been like a game of cat and mouse. Working all day long, pushing all the frustration all out of me. Getting home and seeing her there looking like she was going out of her mind, yet looking more beautiful than she did that morning. I avoided her as much as I could, staying in my room for fear I'd throw her down and kiss the ever-loving shit out of her. I'd wait for her to go to bed before going back on the couch and sleeping. My alarm would ring every two hours. I'd stand there beside her bed sometimes right before I wake her and wonder what it would feel like to lie with her in my arms.

The door opens again, and I look over, hoping it's Amelia. Hoping she came back to finish what we started, but nothing I've ever wanted in my life I actually got. "Dinner is ready." Ethan sticks his head into the garage. I nod at him as he turns around.

You saw what you had to see. Get the fuck out of here. My head yells at me, but my feet, my feet start moving toward the house

When I walk into the kitchen, Kallie is walking out toward the dining room. Following her, I see that everyone is in the dining room sitting down. Jacob sits at the head of the table with Kallie making her way toward the chair on his right. I spot the empty chair right beside Jacob and Ethan. I look toward the other end of the table where Amelia sits between Gabriel and Aubrey. She bends her head to rub noses with Aubrey before turning to Gabriel and picking up his plate. He points at all the food he wants. She places his plate in front of him. "Wait until we say grace." He nods at her. "Give me sugar." She points at her cheek, and he huffs out, leaning over to kiss her cheek.

"Help yourself," Jacob says from beside me. My eyes move from Amelia to the feast in front of me.

Kallie comes back into the room, and the smile on her face is huge. "All that is missing is Graham." She takes a breath. "And the family would be complete."

"That's what you get when you enlist," Ethan says. "He's keeping us safe." Kallie nods at him, and I see that Jacob has put his hand on hers.

"Let's say grace," Jacob says, and I reach out my hands, putting one hand in Ethan's and another in Jacob's. I close my eyes, but I don't listen to the words that are said. Instead, I wonder how different my life would have been had I had this. I stop my head from playing the what-if game as we all say, "Amen."

"Nothing like Mom's cooking," Ethan says, and all eyes go to Emily, who just side-eyes him.

"What? I like your cooking, too."

"Nice save there, McIntyre," Amelia says, pointing her fork at him.

I only talk when someone asks me something. My head is going around and around in circles, and I know I have to get out of here.

"Thank you for dinner," I say to Kallie. "It was delicious as always." I get up, grabbing my empty plate and moving toward the kitchen.

"You don't have to do that, Asher," Kallie says.

Ignoring her, I walk to the kitchen and rinse off my

plate. I open the dishwasher, placing it on the rack, when I suddenly feel eyes on me.

Amelia stands there, wringing her hands in front of her. "Are you headed home?"

"I am," I say, closing the dishwasher and wiping off my hands.

"Can I catch a ride with you?" she asks me softly. "I don't want anyone to go out of their way to bring me home, and I'm a little tired."

"Of course," I say to her, and she turns, walking back to the dining room.

"I'm going to catch a ride with Asher," Amelia says, walking over to Jacob, who pushes back from the table and gets up to hug her. She looks up at him with a smile on her face. "Love you, Dad."

"Love you more, baby girl." He pushes her hair back and kisses her forehead.

"Call me tomorrow," Kallie says to her when she goes to her mother for a hug.

"I'll see you tomorrow," Jacob says to me, his voice loud, making Amelia just look over at me. She moves her eyes from me to her father and then to Ethan.

"Wouldn't miss it," I say to him and turn to walk out of the room when Amelia's voice stops me from moving.

"What am I missing?" she asks, looking all around the room.

I want to tell her nothing, but Jacob is fast to tell her. "I'm trying to convince Asher here to give the police department a chance." He smiles at me.

"Really?" Amelia says, a little shocked.

"It's something I'm thinking about," I finally say.

"First, he has to decide if he wants to stay." Ethan cuts in and slaps my shoulder. "Then we can work on the second part."

"Decides to stay?" Amelia asks me, confusion in her voice, and I don't make eye contact with her.

"I'll see you tomorrow." I ignore her question, nodding as I wait for Amelia to walk out of the house. I hear her footsteps behind me, and I walk over to the truck, opening the door for her. She ignores me, reaching out her hand and pulling the door closed.

I look back at the house, seeing that Jacob and Kallie are standing on the porch watching us. I raise my hand to wave to them and walk around the truck, getting inside.

"You okay?" I ask, and she ignores me, looking out the window and waves to her parents as her face fills with a fake smile. I know it's a fake smile because her eyes don't crinkle at the sides, and her face doesn't light up.

The drive back to her house is brutal, and I look over at her way too many times. Each time, she has her head turned to the side, fixated on looking out the window. She doesn't even wait for me to put the truck in park before she is out.

Putting the truck in park, I get out and look up at the setting sun. I look at the house and then back at the truck. *Get in the truck and leave,* I tell myself. *For you and for her.*

My feet move toward the house. "I'll just get my bags and leave," I tell myself. Opening the door, I walk into the cold house. My eyes look at the couch and find it empty. I walk to the kitchen and open the fridge, grabbing a water bottle. "You're leaving?" I hear her voice and softly close the fridge door.

I look over as she stands there with her arms crossed over her chest. All the words that I have to say are stuck in my throat. "I haven't decided yet" are the only words that come out as I watch her. My feet are glued to the floor instead of going over to her.

"You haven't decided yet." Her voice goes louder. "You haven't decided yet?" she repeats the words like she didn't hear them.

"There are lots of things to process." My eyes never leave hers as she glares at me.

"A lot of things to process," she says. "Really?" Her sarcasm comes out, and I want to laugh at her. I also want to kiss the ever-loving shit out of her. Bury my hands into her hair and claim her mouth with mine. Take the kiss that has been haunting me since I stepped foot into this town.

"I've never stayed in one place longer than four months," I say.

"You've been here longer than that," she says, and I nod silently. "Why would you leave?"

"Why would I stay?" I ask, and she just looks at me, not saying a word. "Exactly." I push off the counter, walking over to my side of the house. "Anyway, it's better to leave before we go past the point of no return."

SOUTHERN SECRETS SOUTHERN

Eighteen

AMELIA

"WHY WOULD I stay?" he asks, and all I can do is stare at him. That almost kiss in the garage made my stomach burn. I didn't think I would be able to walk up the stairs because my whole body was shaking. I sat eating food at the table, the whole time trying not to look over at him. The whole time, I wanted to run outside and scream at the top of my lungs. "Anyway, it's better to leave before we go past the point of no return."

"When are you going to make this decision?" I ask, the lump in my throat getting bigger and bigger.

"As soon as I do, you'll be the first to know," he says, and I know that if I don't walk out right now, he'll see that him leaving will bother me.

Walking to my room, I close the door behind me. I

put my back against it and slowly slip to the floor. *Him leaving would be good*, my head screams. You have one goal and one goal only. To be successful and not count on anyone but yourself. To do it on your own so no one can ever say they gave you anything. Everyone will know I busted my ass to get where I was, and I didn't get there because my family gave it to me.

I ignore him for the next four days, each day waiting for the other shoe to drop.

I SLAM THE door shut and walk over to my grandfather, who stands there with his hands on his hips. "Here she is," he says, looking at me as I make my way over to him. He takes me in his arms and kisses my head. "How are you feeling?"

"All better," I say. "I can go to work tomorrow." Looking to see Christopher and Reed coming out of the barn.

"Hey, you two," I say, walking over to them. "How was last night?"

"Jam-packed," Reed says. "Asher broke up two fights."

I look at him. "Asher?" I question him. "He was there?"

"He's been there the whole time," Reed says. "I like him better than you."

"Screw you." I push his shoulder.

"Did you guys ride?" I ask, and he nods his head.

"We got here early today because Mr. Billy asked us to come and help Asher move some things around the barn."

My head moves to the barn doors as I see the man in question come out of the barn doors. He uses his hand to wipe his forehead. He got home past four o'clock last night and then was out the door before seven this morning. His blue jeans are dirty as fuck, his white T-shirt also dirty but molded to him. He looks up as he walks over and sees me. "Hey." He motions with his head as he walks right past me, going straight to my grandfather. My grandfather smiles at him, and I want to yell out.

Why the fuck are you everywhere I turn?

"Are we going to race?" Christopher asks me, and I turn back to him and nod my head. "Asher saddled your horse before you got here."

"Motherfucker," I mumble under my breath as I walk into the barn and see that my girl is ready to be ridden. My horse looks at me, and I walk over to her. "Why did you allow a stranger to put your saddle on?" I ask her. "Traitor." Grabbing her reins, I walk out of the barn with her to the enclosed fence.

Getting up on her, I look over and see my grandfather standing with my grandmother. His arm is around her as they talk to Asher, who stands there with his legs apart and his arms over his chest. Looking all hot and shit. "What were the fights about last night?" I ask Reed as he joins me.

"One of them thought Asher was trying to get with his girlfriend," Reed says, and my head turns to him.

"Was he?" I ask.

"Not a chance in hell," Christopher says, coming next to us. "He was the one stepping away from her." He shakes his head. "Then there were two blondes who fought over him." He laughs. "I haven't heard squealing like that since two cats got caught in a tree."

I look over at him as he laughs at his own joke. Reed throws his head back and laughs. "Okay, what are we doing?" I ask them.

"Around one time," Reed says. "Best of three."

"You got it," I say, kicking my horse and trotting over to the line.

I get into place, and I look over to see that my grandfather and Asher are watching. I ignore it all as I wait for someone to say go. I push my horse and win; it comes down to the third round. Reed and I are head to head, but my horse loves to win, and I take him with a second. I raise my hands over my head.

"Winner winner chicken dinner." I clap my hands as I get off my horse and walk her back into the barn.

"You got lucky," Reed says, getting off his horse and walking beside me. We put the horses back into the stalls, and I walk over to grab her some water.

"There you are," Chelsea says, coming into the barn. "I've been looking for you."

"There are literally two places I can be." I laugh and walk back to the stall with the bowl of water. "Here or the kitchen."

"Since when do you ever go in the kitchen?" She folds

her arms over her chest. Growing up, she would be in the kitchen with Grandma while I would be dressed just like my grandfather following him around.

"I sometimes go in there," I say, turning to her.

"Name one time?" she asks, and I smile at her.

"When I need to get food." I laugh at my own joke. "Speaking of food," I say, walking out of the stall and locking the door behind me. "Is it ready?"

"Just about," she says as we walk back out of the barn toward the barbecue. "Asher is helping Grandpa with the grill." I groan, and Chelsea laughs and looks over at me. "What is with you?"

"Nothing is up with me," I say, looking around at all the people who are there. All my family is scattered around. My mom is with my aunt Savannah and aunt Olivia as they sit around laughing at something one of them said. My eyes find Asher as he stands by the grill with my grandfather and my brother. "Why is he fucking everywhere I turn?"

"Who is?" she asks me and then follows my eyesight. "Oh, Asher. I thought you liked him."

"Why would you say that?" I ask, shocked. "I will admit that I found him hot when he got here." My mouth never stops. "In a mysterious, *who is this new guy* kind of way." I pause, and she just looks at me. "But …" I point at him. "Now he's integrated himself into the family, and he is fucking everywhere." I look at her. "Say something!" I shriek out.

"I was waiting for you to finish ranting before I said

something." She looks at me. "If you don't like him like that, why did you even invite him to live with you?"

"He isn't living with me." I gasp out, throwing up my hands. "He had no place to go. What was I supposed to do?"

"Umm, literally anything but that." She laughs, and I glare.

"I hate you," I say, turning and storming off away from her.

"Come back here," she says, jogging to catch up with me. "I've never seen you like that." I stop and turn to look at her. "You have never been hung up on any man before."

"What in all of this makes you think I'm hung up on him?" I ask, confused.

"One, you are all jumpy when he is around." She holds up her finger. "Two, you can't stop looking at him when you think no one is looking at you." I scoff out and roll my eyes.

"I do not," I say, and I stop talking when Mayson gets close.

"What are you two talking about?" he asks, and I send her a *don't fucking say anything* look.

"We were wondering if the food was ready?" Chelsea says, putting her arms around his waist.

"They said five minutes," he says.

"Excuse me, I have to wash my hands," I say, walking away from them.

"You can run," Chelsea says, and I turn around, looking at her and walking backward. "But you can't hide." She smiles at me, and when I stick my two fingers up, she puts her head back and laughs.

I stay as far away from him as I can all afternoon. Instead of eating with my cousins because Asher is there, I eat sitting on the grass with Gabriel.

After a couple of hours of playing with the kids, I get up and walk over to say goodbye to my parents and my grandparents. I duck out before anyone sees me, and when I walk into the house, I head straight for the shower.

Dressing in a pair of yoga pants and a T-shirt, I walk back to the kitchen when the front door opens and then slams closed.

"You didn't even tell me you were leaving," Asher says, standing there, his hands on his hips. "I was looking for you all over the place."

"Why didn't you just call my phone?" I ask. His eyes are a deep brown, the same color they turn when he's angry with something.

"Why the hell would I call your phone when we were both at the same place?" he says, huffing out. "I was ready to leave an hour ago, but I was waiting to see if you needed a lift."

"Well, clearly, I made it home okay," I say, opening the water bottle and putting it to my lips. He doesn't say a word to me. All he does is stare. My neck is getting hot. "I heard that you stopped a couple of fights last night," I say, putting one hand on the island.

"Who told you that?" he asks now.

"Are you denying it?" I step away from the counter to walk to the dining room. He stands there not too far away from me. "Someone told me that two girls were fighting over you." My hands start to shake. "Have you decided yet?" I finally cave and ask him the question that I've wanted to ask him ever since I found out he was thinking of leaving.

"Decided what exactly, Amelia?" He says my name, and I hear the whisper of him calling me baby, right before we almost kissed.

"If you are staying or going?" I ask, everything that I told myself all day is out the window. The not knowing has been killing me this whole time.

He walks over to me, standing right in front of me. "This isn't a good idea," he says, his voice going soft toward the end of that sentence. "I know this isn't a good idea. You know that this isn't a good idea." He points at me and then back to himself. "No matter how much I tell myself to get my shit and leave." He steps one step closer to me. "There is always something that stops me from leaving." I swallow now as his scent surrounds me, my stomach flip-flopping. He steps even closer as our chests are touching. "And that someone, Amelia …" His finger trails my cheek. "Is you."

Nineteen

Asher

I TAKE A step even closer as our chests are touching, our breathing in sync. "And that someone, Amelia …" My hand lifts to touch her cheek, to touch any part of her, and her breath hitches when my eyes go from hers to her mouth. "Is you." I admit it to her as well as myself.

"Asher." She lifts her hand and touches my face with her fingertips, and my whole body becomes alive. My eyes look into hers, and my heart soars in my chest. My thumb rubs her cheek, the touch of her skin like silk.

"One chance," I say, and I feel her fingertips move on my cheek. "One last chance." My voice comes out in a whisper, praying like fuck she doesn't say no. Hoping like fuck I can finally get the kiss that has been haunting my dreams.

My palm holds her face, my fingers in her hair, and our eyes meet one last time before I close the gap and take her lips. My hand drops from her face to go around her waist, my head tilting to the side just a touch as our lips meet. I don't know if she lets out a sigh or if I do. My tongue slips into her mouth, and I'm pretty sure this is what heaven would feel like. I'm pretty sure that all the shit that life has handed me was done with this as my reward. I would go through it all over again, just for this one second. Just for this one touch.

Her hand falls from my face to my chest as she kisses me back. I turn my head from one side to the other, and I can't get enough of her. I could spend lifetimes searching for kisses like this.

When I looked around at the barbecue and didn't see her anywhere, I went into a panic. It was almost a full-on panic attack until Ethan saw me looking around like crazy.

"Chill," he said, slapping my shoulder. *"She took off not too long ago."*

"Alone?" I asked, pissed since the threat was still out there. It also didn't help that I hadn't slept more than two hours last night.

Getting in the truck, I ignored that my body was sore. I didn't think about all the times today she walked away from me. I didn't think about sitting down and eating and wishing she was there beside me. I didn't think of any of that as I drove to her house.

Instead, all I could see in my head was the smile she had on her face most of the day. The smile was fake, and anyone who knew her would realize it. The thought that she was upset with me or at me, I just couldn't stomach the latter.

It pushed me off the ledge with whatever little restraint I had. Driving back over here, I tried to calm myself. I tried to talk myself down, but coming into the house and seeing her looking like she did, with her hair down and a surprised look on her face, everything I told myself flew out the window.

I let go of her lips, but I quickly grab her face and pull her back to me. My tongue slips back into her mouth as her tongue slides with mine. Round and round, our tongues fight each other. The kiss gets deeper and deeper. She groans into my mouth and arches her back against me. Her hands going around my neck. "Asher," she says my name breathlessly when I let go of her lips, and then her lips come back to mine. She bites my lower lip; my hands go to her ass. My palms on her ass, I pull her to me. Her head goes back as she feels my cock on her stomach.

She brings her mouth back to me again, and the kiss is harder than the first one. When I feel her hand lifting my shirt, my lips leave hers, and I move one step away from her. Her hands drop from my stomach, and my hands drop from her ass. "I'm sorry," I say to her, and her eyes open. Her eyes are a deep blue, her lips plump. "I shouldn't have done that." My heart wants to come out of my fucking chest as it pounds. "I shouldn't have just kissed you."

She blinks a couple of times. "I kissed you back," she

says, her hand coming up to touch her lips. Her middle finger traces her bottom lip. If you look close enough, you can see little red dots that my beard left.

"If I didn't kiss you, would you have kissed me?" I ask, and I shake my head. "Don't answer that." I don't want to know the answer. Whatever the answer is, I can't be the man who deserves her.

"No," she says softly. "I wouldn't have kissed you."

"Well, there you have it," I say, running my hands through my hair as I swallow down the lump in my throat. Even she knew I wasn't worth this. If I didn't think I had to leave before, I definitely think it's time to go now. I turn, walking toward the bedroom.

"Just like that?" she snaps at me, and I turn to look at her. Her chest rises and falls with one hand on her stomach. "So just like that, you come in here." She uses her other hand to point at the floor in front of her. "And kiss the ever-loving shit out of me." Her voice goes louder. "And then just say you're sorry?"

"I don't know what else to say," I say.

"Why did you kiss me?" she asks.

"I couldn't stop myself," I say. "I've been dreaming of kissing you since I first met you. Since you smiled at me the first time and extended your hand out to me." I replay the first day we met. "You were wearing jeans and a white shirt. Your hair was tied on the top of your head. You reached out and smiled at me with your hand extended, and all you said was, 'I'm Amelia.'" She just stares at me. "From that moment, I've wanted to kiss you," I admit. "From that moment, I fought kissing you every single day."

"But …" she says and shakes her head.

"I'm not the man you deserve," I say, the burning in my stomach feeling like my body is on fire. Like the poison in me is burning on the inside trying to get out.

"I never said that," she says, blinking away the tears in her eyes. "Not once did I ever say that."

"You don't have to." I laugh bitterly. "Being here, being around your family. I know that I have nothing to offer you. I have nothing to offer anyone." My heart beats so fast in my chest I don't know what to say. "There are things about me you don't know."

"There are things about me you don't know either," she says as one lone tear runs down her face.

My mouth is getting dry as my heart screams for her. "There are parts of me irrecoverably broken." Her hand flies to her chest, and I would give anything to feel her heart under my hand. "We are from two different worlds," I say, and for the first time in my life, I tell my story to someone.

"From the story my mother told me, she was sixteen when I was born." I tell her the story, my eyes never leaving hers. "Sixteen. She didn't even have a mother herself. She was in a foster home when she met this guy who promised her the world. She was a waitress at a local diner. He came in one day, and she knew right away he wasn't from there. The thick gold watch on his wrist, along with the brand-new SUV he drove made them both know they were from two different parts of the world. She didn't think twice about him, and the next day, he came back, and this time, they started talking." I shake my head. "One thing led to another, and she got pregnant. He stopped showing up. She finally tracked him down, and when she told him she was pregnant, he laughed at her."

"Asher," she says my name.

"That's not even the worst part. She had me, and it wasn't an easy delivery. The doctor gave her pain pills, and she got addicted." My voice goes softer. "Having me killed her." I admit one of my biggest secrets that I've never told a soul. Not even my foster brother.

"You can't believe that." She takes a step forward.

"If she didn't have me, who knows where she would be," I say. "She tried." I think back, and if I close my eyes and concentrate just hard enough, I can see her face. "She tried to kick the habit, but one thing after another kicked her back, and then she was hanging around with another guy who promised her the world." I look down. "I was in foster care for three days, and she was sitting in a morgue. I didn't attend her funeral because there was no one to pay for one. They got me dressed up one day, and I thought I was going to be adopted. I didn't even know what that meant, but I knew kids said when they dress you up, they take you to your new family. Not me, they got me dressed up to take me to court to officially say I was a ward of the state. My grandmother showed up for five seconds to sign her rights over. My mom looked so much like her when I saw her, I cried 'mom' after her."

"Oh my God," she says, putting her hand to her mouth, the tears staining her cheeks. I should stop. I should stop right now and not tell her the rest. But the flood gates have opened, and everything wants to come out.

"And that was the good part of my life," I say. "I was in and out of foster homes, never staying at one too long. I was treated like a waste of space. I was told time and time again that all I was, was a paycheck. Stay quiet and don't mess this up for us." I swallow. "When you are told your whole life that no one wants you and that you aren't worth anything, you start to believe it. Even if I didn't want to believe it, the kids at school were good at telling me that I was nothing since I came from a foster house."

"You are worth so much," she says, and I just shake my head.

"I went five days with only eating a loaf of bread," I say. "My foster mother was in Mexico. She left a ten-year-old for five days with a loaf of bread. No one would have known had the apartment downstairs not flooded. You grow up fast, that's for sure. When I was thirteen, my foster father climbed into bed with me." I watch her face. "Lucky for me, I always went to bed dressed in all my clothes. Also lucky for me, I learned to yell real loud. Then I met Ryan, and the two of us made a plan to take off. We lived on the streets for six months. We had each other's back, and then he got sick. I worked my ass off to make sure he was okay, but it wasn't good enough; nothing was good enough. I couldn't even rent a room for him to die in a bed. Instead, he died in a crack house with people doing meth around him." She swallows as my own tears fall from my eyes. "You learn two things in foster care. One, no one is going to protect you like you, and two, only the strong will survive."

"You survived," she says. "You are the strongest person I know."

"I survived by running," I tell her. "Survived by never staying in one place for too long. Living paycheck to paycheck by the skin of my teeth." The weight of my past still presses on my shoulders. "That's the man you just kissed," I tell her, leaving out the fact I'm hiding the biggest secret not only from her but also her whole family, and it's eating me up inside.

She wipes the tear that runs down her face, and I want to go to her so much, but I know it's just prolonging the inevitable. "I'll get my things."

SOUTHERN SECRETS SOUTHERN

Twenty

AMELIA

"I'LL GET MY things," he says and turns to walk away, his shoulders slumped and his head down. This man who is worth so much yet doesn't see it.

"Stop," I snap, taking one step forward. He turns around, and my eyes meet his. The look of defeat is all over his face. "You don't get to do this," I say, my hands shaking, and I really wish I could sit down. "You don't get to give me all that and not listen to what I have to say."

"Amelia," he says my name in a broken plea. "Just." I hold up my hand to stop him from talking. I hold up my hand, and he sees it shaking. He takes a step forward, but I shake my head. I can't do this if he's next to me.

"I know a man who woke up at the ass crack of dawn

to go out to help an old man fix his fence. An old man he isn't even related to, I might add." I shake my head. "I know this man who lost everything and was sadder because of the impact that loss had on my family. I know a man who puts other people before himself. I know this man who would give anyone the shirt off his back." I stand straight and pull my shoulders back. "There are things about me that you don't know either," I say, and he just looks at me. "Things no one knows. And I mean no one. Not my parents, not my grandfather, not even Chelsea."

"You don't have to do this," he says, but after everything he gave me tonight, I owe him this right now.

"I don't have to but"—I look down at my hands—"I want you to know." I swallow the fear that he might look at me differently. "I fell in love when I was fourteen years old. He worked for my grandfather, doing stuff around the barn and then he was the up-and-coming rodeo champion. He trained with my cousins, and there was no denying he was going to be a champion. He was two years older than me." I ignore the pain forming in my heart. "One night, I found him alone in the barn, and we started talking. Then slowly, we would spend more time together. In secret, of course. No way would he even acknowledge me when any of my family members were around. When I was fifteen, he gave me my first kiss." I wipe the tear away, the memories that I've kept in a locked box coming out.

"Of course, he made me promise not to tell a soul." Just thinking about it, I was so stupid. "He had me convinced that my grandfather would fire him if he knew and that my family would block him from becoming the rodeo champ. So, for three years, we hid our relationship, or whatever it is that you want to call it. I would sneak out of my house and meet him at the barn. It was stupid, so fucking stupid." I laugh, putting my hand to my forehead as I shake my head. "I didn't tell a soul. Not one fucking soul. Not my mother, not my grandfather, not even Chelsea and Quinn." I hold up my hand with my finger up. "He was my secret and only mine. We would stay up all night sometimes as he spoke about his big dream of owning his own farm and being rodeo champ. Everything that he wanted to achieve with me by his side. Every single time he mentioned his dream, I was the one beside him holding his hand." The tears come. "I loved him so much that his dream became my dream. I would have followed him anywhere." I shake my head. "I was going to leave everything that I know and love just for him. Because he was my everything."

"Amelia," he says my name softly.

"I know, stupid, right? Who the fuck falls in love when they are fifteen?" I laugh as the tears pour down my face. "I mean, besides my parents and my grandparents and my aunt Savannah and my uncle Beau." He smiles softly as he looks at me.

I gather the strength to continue, knowing that the next part will take me back to a place I never wanted to go. There was never a need to tell anyone this, but I want Asher to know. I want to give him a piece of myself that he just gave me. "The plan was that he was going to get us a place, and the minute I turned eighteen, we would get married. Every single weekend, he would head down and see if there was anything we could afford. Then he would come back and tell me all about the apartments he looked at and how it was going to be perfect for us." I put my hand to my stomach, feeling like I'm going to be sick. I take a second, the lump in my throat getting bigger and bigger. Even though I told myself he would never get another tear from me.

"I counted down the days. Counted down the hours until the day I turned eighteen. He had been gone a week. He was fixing up our place, he said, and putting the final touches on it. He even sent me pictures." The hurt is like it was yesterday instead of years ago. "The night I turned eighteen, I didn't sleep a wink. Not one fucking second. I was so excited for him to come and get me. I was on pins and needles all day. I couldn't wait to finally tell everyone about us. I was so excited to finally do all the things I dreamed of doing with him. Walking into my parents' house. Holding his hand. Kissing him when I wanted. Finally able to show everyone that I found someone I was going to spend the rest of my life with. My parents threw me this ridiculous party with everyone there." I close my eyes as my heart shatters yet again in my chest. "His truck got there. I got up with a huge smile on my face as I saw him get out of the driver side. I was one second from running to him when I saw the passenger door open. My feet were stuck to the ground. This woman climbed out of the truck, and he held out his hand for her, and together they walked into my party." I look into his brown eyes, feeling all the warmth that a hug could give from one look. "He introduced his new wife to everyone." Saying the words almost cut me off at the knees. I put my hand out onto the table. "He was married." I take a deep breath in. "He was married to someone else."

I close my eyes again, and this time, I feel his arms around me. "Baby," he says softly. "Don't cry."

My arms go around his neck as I bury my face into his neck. "It's why I'll never give anyone control. It's why I won't let anyone pay for anything. It's why I work two jobs. It's why my dreams are mine and mine alone. It's why I have to do this myself. It's as much for me as a *fuck you* to him," I say, laughing.

"He doesn't deserve your tears," Asher says, kissing my forehead. "He doesn't deserve to have any space in your head." His voice goes lower. "He had perfection in his hand, and he let it go." His voice is almost a whisper.

My head comes out from his neck, his eyes on mine. "Amelia," he says my name, and this time, it's me who makes the first step. My hand comes out, and I finally touch his face the way I've wanted to touch it since I met him. The stubble from his beard is pricking my hand. "You," I say, smiling. "You are the only one who's tempted me." My fingers go to his lips, touching his bottom lip that I want to kiss. "The only one I've ever let myself dream of having." I move my nose with his, softly side to side. "You were everywhere." The tears roll down my cheeks, past the smile that has formed on my face. "And I mean everywhere." It's his turn to smile.

"It pissed me off so much. I fought with Chelsea today about it," I admit. "You got under my skin, Asher."

"I didn't mean to," he says softly, and I lean in, kissing his lips softly. Once, twice, and then on the third time, his hand goes to the back of my head, and he tilts his head to the side. My mouth opens, and his tongue slides into my mouth.

Home.

It's the only thing that comes to mind when our tongues tangle. I kiss him until I'm breathless. I kiss him with everything that I have. I kiss him, afraid I'll never get to kiss him again.

"I don't want to stop kissing you," he says, "but …" My eyes open to see him staring at me. His eyes are the color of a rich whiskey. I could spend all night getting lost in them. "I need to take a shower." He kisses me again. "I have dust and sweat all over me." I step out of his arms, and I feel this draft rush up my body, and I shiver. "Don't go anywhere," he says, and I laugh. He turns around to walk to the bathroom, stopping and then turning back to me. "He's an idiot." Everything in me stops. "For leaving you." Shaking his head, he smiles. "I mean, if I ever get to meet him, I might thank him." He smirks.

"For what?" I ask, confused.

"For giving me a chance to have the best kiss I've had in my whole life." He turns toward his bathroom. Only when I hear his door close do I finally breathe properly.

"I guess I should thank him, too," I say finally. "Because I just had a kiss I will never forget."

Twenty-One

Asher

THE SOFT SOUND of the alarm wakes me up along with her voice. "What is that sound?" I hear her mumble, and I smile when I feel her snuggle up against me. Her leg hitches over my hips as she puts her head on my chest. "Make it stop," she says, and I lean over and grab my phone off the top of the couch, shutting off the alarm. Her hair tickles my nose as she buries her face in my neck. "I'm fine," she says, and I laugh.

Last night, I walked into this house not expecting to show her all of me. I expected her to change the way she looked at me. I expected to see some disgust that the person staying in her house slept on the fucking street. She didn't. Instead, she shared with me her deepest, darkest secret. A secret I know killed her to tell me, killed her to relive it.

I watched her struggle through it until I could no longer just stand there and not have her in my arms. When I got out of the shower, I expected to find the house dark and her in her bedroom. What I got was her sitting in the middle of the couch with her feet curled under her and her hair pinned on her head, watching some show on television. I sat next to her and all I did was look over at her and my hands had a mind of their own. My hands got buried in her hair, and we spent the night on the couch making out like a couple of crazy teenagers.

"What time is it?" she mumbles, and I look down, seeing that her eyes are still closed.

"Two," I tell her, and she groans. "If that phone rings again in two hours." I turn her on her side, and my mouth covers hers. Whatever she was going to say was swallowed by our kiss. I spent all night kissing her, and every single time, it felt like the first time.

"Sleep," I say. Opening her eyes, she rubs her nose on my chin and smells me before kissing me softly and putting her head back in the crook of my neck. I want to watch her sleep, but with her in my arms, I fall asleep faster than I ever have.

When the alarm rings again, I know it's time for me to get up. "Baby," I say softly. "I have to get up."

"Okay," she says, and she doesn't move.

"You need to get off me." I laugh. When I woke up this time, she had rolled on me. I turn her toward the back of the couch and get up.

"It's cold," she says, and I grab the throw and place it

on her. "No," she says. "Come back."

"I wish I could," I say, bending down and kissing her. "But I need to get to work." I walk to the kitchen and start the coffee machine before going to the bedroom and getting dressed. My cock is hard like a rock as I smell her all around me.

I look at the couch when I walk out and see it empty. "I made you coffee," she says, holding up a to-go cup while she sips the cup of coffee in her own hand.

"Why didn't you go back to bed?" I ask, grabbing the cup. "It's early," I say, seeing that it's just past five.

"Where are you going so early?" she asks.

"I work out with your father and brother," I say.

"Since when?" she asks, shocked.

"Something that they roped me into last week." I take a sip of the coffee. "They want to see if I would pass the physical part of police training."

Her hand goes to the counter as she puts her cup down. "Have you decided if you are going to do that?"

"No." I shake my head. "But it can't hurt to be prepared for it if I do." I walk to her and put my finger under her chin. "Kiss me," I say. With a smile, she turns to me and wraps her arms around my shoulders, getting on her tippy-toes. She tilts her head to the side and gives me the kiss I asked for. Her tongue slides with mine, and even if I don't try to deepen it, it does anyway.

The phone in my pocket rings, letting me leave her lips. Pulling the phone out of my pocket, I bring it to my ear without looking to see who it was. "Hello," I say, and she tilts her head back as she kisses my neck.

"Asher, it's Jacob." I step back as if someone threw a pail of ice water on me. "Everything okay?"

"Yeah," I say, looking around. "Why?"

"You're usually the one opening the gym for us," he says, laughing.

"I'm on my way," I say. "Be there in ten."

I disconnect the call and put the phone back in my pocket. "That was your father." I look at her. "I need to go." I turn to walk away. "How do I look?"

"Um, good?" she says, smirking. "Why?"

"Does it look like I spent the night making out with his daughter?" I ask, and she brings the cup of coffee up to her lips.

"No." She shakes her head. "But he's going to wonder who you have a hard-on for." She rolls her lips when I look down and see my cock straining to get the fuck out.

"Fuck," I say, looking down, then turning and walking out of the room. "You are going to get me in trouble," I mumble.

"Who are you talking to?" she asks me, and I look over my shoulder at her. "Me or the cock."

"Trouble!" I yell as I walk out the door to my truck. I open the truck door and stop when I see everything in the glove box out. The hair on the back of my neck sticks up. I look in the back and the seats are cut down the middle.

I take the phone out and call Jacob. "Are you stuck?"

"Someone vandalized my truck," I say, looking around to see if I see anything out of the ordinary. I walk toward Amelia's truck and see that her door is open slightly. "Amelia's looks like it was broken into also."

"Be there in ten," he says, and I run back inside. My heartbeat feels like it's going to explode in my chest. My mouth gets drier than the desert on a summer day.

"Amelia!" I shout her name, scared that someone got into the house when I walked out. "Amelia!" My voice is frantic, and she comes running out of her bedroom in her bra and panties.

"What's the matter?" Fear is in her voice. Everything in my head is jumbled when I see her standing in front of me. Her hand to her chest, her face white. "What happened?" she says, and the sound of rocks crunching makes me snap out of it.

"Go get dressed. Your father is here," I say, my voice tight, and she nods and turns to walk back into her room.

"Asher?" I hear Jacob call my name.

"In here," I say, and he comes in wearing his workout gear. "I'm not leaving her alone," I say, and he nods at me.

Amelia comes out of her room wearing shorts and a shirt. . Her face is still white, though, and I can tell she is scared. "What's going on?" she asks, looking at me and then her father.

"Truck has been vandalized, and I think yours has been messed with also," I say, and she raises her hand to her chest.

"Let's go check it out," Jacob says, and he turns to walk out of the house. She follows her father, but I grab her hand, and she turns to look at me.

"Are you okay?" I ask, and she nods her head, but I know that she isn't. "It's okay to say you aren't."

"Fine," she says. "I'm pissed." I just watch her as she steps closer to me, and her voice goes lower. "I'm pissed that instead of spending the day thinking about us kissing, you're going to be all in detective mode." I stare at her in shock. "Now, before my father comes back in, let's get out there."

I follow her outside and find Jacob and Ethan there. "Amelia's car looks like they only checked the glove compartment and the trunk," Ethan says. "But yours." He looks at me. "They were looking for something."

I walk to the truck and take another look. "Do you think anything is missing?" Jacob asks as I look at all the papers on the floor.

"I have never even looked in the glove compartment," I tell them. "It's Billy's old truck. I wasn't going to snoop in his things." I look in the back seat and see the papers that I keep there for the farm are scattered all over the place, but the big cut down the middle shows that they were looking for something.

"Casey is going through the feed," Jacob says. He props the phone to his ear as he relays what Casey is saying. "Happened at three a.m." I look over at Amelia, who stands there watching her father. "Two guys. One for each car. Faces are covered. Okay, perfect," he says, hanging up.

"From now on, you don't come here alone." I look at Amelia. "Not to the barn, not to the bar. Not anywhere."

She rolls her eyes at me, and if her father and brother weren't here, I would kiss the ever-loving shit out of her. "He's right," Jacob says. "From now on, I want us all to be on alert. Everyone." He looks over at Ethan. "It's time to get everyone involved."

"But we don't even know anything," Amelia says, and her father looks at her.

"We know enough that two people were outside of your house when you were in your bed sleeping," he tells her, and I swallow down my guilt. "I'm not taking any chances with you."

"I'll get her at the bar." I speak up. "And I'll come back in the morning and get her to bring her to the barn."

"We can take turns in the morning," Ethan says. "You have the nights since you live with her."

It takes us an hour to get everything cleaned up, and Kallie comes over and makes sure that Amelia is taken to the barn.

I get into the truck and make my way over to the barn that holds all the tools. Billy is there waiting for me. "Sorry," I say as I get out. "For being late." He walks over to the truck with his hat on his head. If I ever wanted to be someone in my life, it would be Billy.

He shakes his head and laughs. "Only you would be apologizing for being late because someone broke into your truck."

"I'll start everything in a second," I say. "I just need some duct tape," I say, walking into the barn, going straight to the shed that holds all the things I need.

"What are you going to do with that?" he asks, and I look back over at him.

"They sliced the back seat," I say, walking back to the truck and opening the back door to the back seat. "I'm going to tape the seats shut."

Billy looks at me as I start to peel some of the silver tape. "Can you hold this?"

He shakes his head at me. "Are you out of your mind, son?" The way he calls me son gets me every single time. Nobody has ever called me that, and the first time he called me that, I had to blink away tears.

"What?" I ask, looking back at him. "It'll work."

"That truck is twenty years old," he reminds me. "I taught my grandkids to drive in this truck."

I huff out. "I'm so sorry, Billy."

He slaps me on the shoulder. "Do you know how many times Charlotte has asked me to get rid of this truck?"

"It still works fine," I say, and he throws his head back and laughs. I hear the sound of rocks crunching, and when I look up, Casey's driving a strange truck.

He gets out of the truck and looks at his father and then me. "Hey," he says, raising his chin. "What do you have there?"

"Asher is duct-taping the back seat," Billy says, laughing, and Casey shakes his head.

"Here," he says, tossing me a set of keys, my hand coming out and catching them. "It's time that you got a new car anyway." I stand here shocked as I look down at the keys in my hand and then back at Casey.

"I don't need a new truck," I tell them. "I can't take this." I look over at them and then back to the truck that looks brand new.

"Yeah, that's what Jacob said you would say," Casey tells me. "He also said to tell you that you are going to be driving his daughter, and he doesn't want her in that death trap."

"I don't know what to say." I look at them, my mouth becoming dry and my hands shaking as I look down at the black key. "I can't pay for this truck," I admit.

"No one is asking you to pay for shit, boy. You show up every single day and work your ass off. You show up even when no one expects you to. Heck, you even showed up when I told you not to show your face," Billy says, and I laugh.

"I think you said if I showed up, you'd fire my ass," I remind him.

"Of course, he did," Casey says, laughing and shaking his head.

I look over at Billy, and there is nothing that I can say right now, the smile on his face is so big. "You've earned this."

Twenty-Two

AMELIA

"WHERE IS YOUR bodyguard?" Reed jokes, walking behind the bar. Emptying the bin of ice, he's carrying it into the freezer as we get ready for the Saturday night rush. "Usually, I have to ask permission to enter." I push his shoulder, and he laughs. "The truth hurts."

"I'm going to hurt you if you keep talking," I say, and that makes him laugh even harder.

"Momma said I'm not allowed to hit girls," Reed says.

"And if you do, I'm going to kick your ass," Quinn says, and I look over at him. "And then I'm going to tell Mom, and she's going to kick your ass."

Reed smirks over at him. "Not her baby," he says, walking away, and I look back at Quinn. We both watch him walk out, and then he turns and winks over at a group of girls who have been watching him. They all sigh when he walks by, and Quinn and I look at each other and laugh.

"He's going to give my mother white hair," Quinn says, and I lean on the bar with both hands outstretched, laughing.

The night is just starting, and I watch as the crowd grows. I look over at the door and see Asher walk in and my stomach literally flips. I watch him laugh with Ethan and then shake his head. I stop for a second and just watch him even though I saw him less than two hours ago when he dropped me off here and waited until Reed showed up. Dressed in dark blue jeans, he shows off just a bit of what he has to offer. After feeling it on my leg, I can say it's exactly how I thought it would be. A white T-shirt is under the blue-and-white-checkered long-sleeve shirt rolled up to his elbows. His black hair looks like he just ran his hand through it, and his eyes look up as if he knows I'm watching. His brown eyes light up just like the smile that fills his face. He gives me a chin up as he makes his way over to the bar.

The last week has been crazy, to say the least. They still haven't found the two guys who broke into our cars. He is there in the morning and doesn't leave until someone else arrives, and then every single night, he shows up at the bar and helps me close it. To anyone watching, it would be like two friends, but when we get into the house, we waste no time lunging for each other. I spend every single night in his arms. We spend the night torturing each other with kisses. I wait for his touch, my body yearning for it.

"Um." I hear him say when he walks behind the bar. "You changed?" He does the once-over up and down.

"You didn't think I would wear yoga pants?" I ask, shaking my head. I came in wearing yoga pants and a sweater, but I'm wearing a pair of jean shorts that are loose and hang on my hips with a thin brown and silver country belt. A white tank top with two horseshoes on the center, hang loose.

"Here," he says, taking off his long-sleeve shirt and handing it to me.

"What am I supposed to do with that?" I ask, and he looks around to make sure no one is watching our exchange. He leans in, and I smell the woodsy smell that is him. My heart speeds up, thinking he's going to kiss me.

His mouth goes to my ear. "If you don't tie this around your waist, I'm going to have to kiss the shit out of you in front of all these people so they know you're off-limits." He pushes back after he finishes talking.

"Is that so?" I fold my arms over my chest. I've never had someone be territorial about me before.

"What does a girl have to do to get a drink around here?" Chelsea says, making me look at her. I turn back to look at Asher, who holds the shirt from his finger.

"Your choice," he says, and I grab his shirt and tie it around my waist, and he glares at me.

"Compromise," I say and turn away from him as I walk to the end of the bar.

"What's going on there?" Chelsea says, motioning with her chin.

"Nothing. I dirtied my shorts," I say. "What do you want to drink?" I look around to see that the place is jam-packed. "It's going to be another crazy night." I smile. "You know what that means."

"No," Chelsea says. "But I'm sure you'll tell me." She has to yell the last part of the sentence.

The DJ for the night has started the music as Luke Bryan starts singing "Country Girl." I put my hands up as I dance down the bar to get her a beer.

I don't have time to talk to her or anyone else for that matter as we work to get everyone served. I work side by side with Asher, and I try to ignore his little touches when he walks past me. His hand on my lower back. His hands grabbing my hips when he reaches over me. It is driving me crazy. It also makes me play the same game he is playing.

My hand slowly slips from his back to his ass as I work around him. He looks at me sideways, and I see him squeezing his fist. One time, I walk over to him and get on my tippy-toes behind him, my tits squeezing into his back. "Two can play that game, Asher," I whisper into his ear and then quickly walk back over to my side of the bar.

The two of us working side by side laughing is one of the best nights I've had at work. I sing songs at the top of my lungs and all he will do is shake his head and serve the next person.

"Why are you so happy?" Chelsea looks over at me

when things finally get quiet.

"What do you mean?" I ask, avoiding her eyes. I haven't told anyone about Asher, and I am afraid with just one look, she is going to know I'm lying.

"I mean the whole singing and laughing and joking," she says. "And the whole tits on his back." She points over at Asher, who is wiping down the bar on his side.

"He was in the way." I try to hide the shock that she picked up on that. I look over at her as she sits there alone since everyone bailed out five minutes ago. She is waiting for Mayson to come back from the bathroom.

"Really?" She almost sings the word. "Interesting."

"Don't start with that tone," I say, hating the fact she is teasing me.

"FYI." She gets up when she sees Mayson making his way back. "Seeing you that happy looks good on you."

I roll my eyes. "There is nothing going on." I fold my arms over my chest.

"Oh, if that's the case, there is someone who just started working with me," she says. "I was thinking of setting her up with Asher." I glare at her, and she claps her hands together and throws her head back and laughs as loud as she can.

"You're an asshole." I grab the glass off the bar.

"I wasn't finished with that," she says and then turns to Mayson, wrapping her arms around his neck. "It's time for you to take your woman home." She kisses him on the lips and then turns back to look at me. "See you tomorrow."

I nod at her, looking over at Asher who stands there

watching me. "What?" I ask, and he walks over to me.

"Hi," he says softly with a sly smile, and I lean back on the bar.

"Hi," I say, and my hand comes up on its own and goes to the middle of his chest. The heat from his chest seeps into me, and his brown eyes shimmer.

"You good?" he asks. His hand comes up and pushes my hair behind my ear.

"Tired but good," I say as my hand slips off him when someone steps up to the bar. His hand falls to his side.

"Only two hours to go," he says, walking away from me, and I laugh.

People slowly start to leave, and before I know it, I look up and it's empty. Reed and Christopher are picking up the last of the stray empty glasses.

The music plays softly as I clean up the bar. "I'm going to help the boys bring out the garbage."

"Okay," I say, drying up a couple of glasses and making sure that everything is in its place.

"I'm out," Dolly says, coming over to me, bringing her black bag. "I always think we are never going to top the weekend before, and then bam, it blows it out of the water." I smile, looking at the empty bar. "You did good."

"Thank you," I say. "See you Monday."

I walk over to the sports section and turn off the lights. Making my way toward the pool tables, I make sure everything is cleaned up.

I step out and see Asher walking back in. "Where are the boys?" I ask, walking toward him and meeting him in the middle of the dance floor.

"Told them to take off," he says, and his hand grabs my hand and pulls me to him. He wraps his arm around my waist and slowly lowers his lips to mine. My tongue comes out eagerly to meet his, and my hands go to his chest as I kiss him back. He lets my lips go softly. "I waited all night to do that," he says softly, pushing the hair from my face. "There is also something I've wanted to do all night." He lets me go, walking over to the radio on the stage. Taking out his phone, he plugs it in and the song, "Cowboys like Me," plays through the speakers, filling the room. Turning, he walks toward me with a smile, and his eyes turn a soft brown. My stomach flips, and a smile fills my face. He holds out his hand when he reaches me. "Dance with me."

Twenty-Three

Asher

"DANCE WITH ME." I hold out my hand to her. I don't know what I'm doing because I've never been in this position. I've never been with someone I couldn't wait to see again. I haven't been with someone who causes a sense of peace to wash over me as soon as I see her.

She places her small hand into mine, and I pull her to me, smashing our chests together. "I didn't know you were a dancer." I wrap an arm around her waist while she puts one hand around my shoulder. I look down at her smiling face, her eyes turning soft blue right before my eyes.

"I don't dance," I say as we turn around in a circle. "If we are being honest." The words come out so low I don't know if she can hear them.

She stops moving, and I can sense her whole body going stiff. "Being dishonest is not an option between us." The words come out curt and direct.

"I know," I whisper. She nods her head, and I can feel her relaxing in my arms again. "Like I was saying …" I kiss her forehead as we turn around in a circle. "I've never danced with anyone before," I admit. The thought of her in someone else's arms is almost too much to bear.

She looks up at me. "Are you saying I'm your first?" she jokes, tilting her head back, her index finger coming to rub my cheek. My head turns to catch her finger with a kiss.

"I'm saying you are the first girl who I've ever danced with. You are the first girl I've wanted to dance with," I admit.

"I'll take it." She laughs. I bend my head, and she tilts her head back, waiting for my kiss. My mouth lowers to hers. My hand moves from her hand to her neck, intertwining my fingers in her hair. Her tongue comes out to slide with mine. Her hand falls to my hip, her thumb holding the side of my jeans. The arm around my shoulder comes down to hold my arm, her touch like an electric shock bringing me to life. I close my mouth and open it again, my tongue coming out to seek hers. She moans into my mouth, and it shoots straight to my cock. Her hand goes to the back of my neck as her fingers go into my hair.

The song ends, and all you can hear in the dimly lit bar is the sound of us kissing. My head moves to the other side, deepening the kiss. My lips let hers go, and

I rub her nose gently with mine. Our chests are pressed against each other. "Another thing I was dying all night to do." I kiss her lips. "Is kiss you."

"Really?" She kisses under my chin. "What else have you been dying to do?" she asks me in a wicked way. This past week has been pure torture for me, lying with her and kissing the shit out of her.

"Other things I can't say," I joke, kissing her lips and then moving the kisses to her cheek and then to her neck. The smell of lavender is still on her. "So many other things."

She giggles, and it's like music to my ears. Even more so, it's hurting the fuck out of my cock that is restricted by my jeans. "Really?" She bends back to see my eyes, and I love the color of her eyes when she's playful. They are a crystal blue, and in her left eye is one little speck of dark. "I've been thinking of other things also." I stop moving as I look at her. My hand drops from her neck, and we stand in front of each other. Her long tanned legs are on show, and when I saw her outfit tonight, it took everything in me not to cover her up. When she turned around to grab something, I made sure to stand in front of her, even though she was wearing my shirt around her waist and you couldn't see anything.

"Amelia," I say her name in more of a plea, looking up at the ceiling.

"I've been thinking about …" She wraps her arms around my waist and kisses my neck softly. "About kissing you." She moves over to the other side of my neck and kisses me, driving me fucking mad. All I want to do is bury my hands in her hair and then drag her to the middle of the floor and have my way with her.

"I'm hanging on by a thread," I say, my hands on her hips to force her not to move any closer to me or else I'll shoot off like a kid.

"Tell me what you're thinking about?" she asks, her voice so soft.

"That's not fair." I look down at her.

"Why?" she asks, and her hands slide under the hem of my shirt, making me hiss.

"Because," I say, trying to focus on anything but the way her hands feel on me.

"Fine, I'll go first," she says. "I want to kiss you in places no one can see."

I groan and take a step back as I look at her. "You have no idea what you do to me."

"Tell me?" she whispers.

"You drive me crazy," I finally huff out. "Kissing you is what I think about doing all day long." I put my hands on my hips. "All day, every day. I want to lay you down and kiss every single inch of you. I want to claim every single part of you. I want to put my mark on you so bad. I want to go out and know that under your clothes, you have my mark." I watch her eyes to see if it's too much for her. I watch her eyes to see if she feels the same way I do. "I want to take you home and make love to you." I finally say the words I've been dying to say, my heart beating so loud it echoes in my ears. "That is what I've thought about. I want you, Amelia."

She looks at me, and then she blinks, and her hand

comes up to wipe the tear before it runs down her face. My stomach sinks in fear that I've scared her in some way or another, so I reach out for her, cupping her face with my hands. "I'm sorry," I say, my thumbs rubbing her cheeks.

"No one …" she says and looks down, but I move her face up with my hands.

"Don't hide from me," I say. "Whatever you do, don't hide from me."

She starts over. "No one has ever said that to me." Her hand cups my cheek. "No one has ever wanted me that bad."

I kiss her lips softly. At this moment, nothing would stop me from kissing her. The fear seeps into my bones that there will come a time when she won't want me. There will be a time when the rest of my baggage comes to light, and just knowing she won't want me anymore is enough to crush my soul. But we have this, and this is our time. Everything from the outside is unimportant right now. For once in my fucking life, I'm going to do something for me. I'm selfish enough to know that what I'm taking will never be mine, but for today, for tonight, for next week, I'm going to pretend I'm just a man who wants a woman.

"Asher," she whispers.

"Yeah, baby?" I answer, and she smiles shyly.

"I like that you call me that," she admits, and I smile as she walks out of my arms.

I watch her walk to the stage, climbing on it and grabbing my phone. I watch her walk to the back as she goes into the office.

My whole body is on edge, thinking about what she is doing. Wondering if I pushed her too far and worried that she would look at me differently. She comes out with her purse in her hand, and the clicking of her cowboy boots on the floor echoes in the empty bar. She holds out her hand to me. "Take me home," she says, putting her hand in mine.

I bring our hands up to my mouth and kiss her fingers. I hold her hand the whole time she turns off the rest of the lights. We don't say anything as she locks the door, and I walk to the truck. I open the door for her and help her in, then walk to my side. She holds my hand while I drive to her house.

I put the truck in park and look over at her. She is looking down at her hands in her lap. "Talk to me," I say.

Her hand reaches for the handle of the truck, and she opens it. I follow her out, and when we get to her front door, she unlocks it and walks in. She waits for me to enter before closing the door behind her. "I didn't want to do this outside," she says, "because I know the cameras are watching."

I'm so mesmerized by her that I didn't even think about the cameras outside. The only thing I could think about was her and what was going through her mind. "I didn't even think of that," I say honestly, and she comes to me. My back is against the door, and the only light is coming from the small side table lamp in the living room.

Her hand comes up to touch my chest, the palm of

her hand flat against my chest. She can feel my heart pounding. "I want it," she says softly. "Everything you said." Her hand moves from my chest to my shoulder. "All the things you said you wanted to do to me." She swallows. "I want to do them. I want to kiss you until you snap and take me." She steps in just a touch more, and our chests are almost touching. "I want you to take me to bed." Her nose nuzzles my neck, and then she kisses me softly. My whole body melts under her touch.

"I want to worship you," I finally say, my voice trembling. "I want to worship every part of you."

I look into her eyes as she takes the step to close the distance between us. Two words is all it takes for me to finally snap. "I'm yours."

Twenty-Four

Amelia

I TAKE THE biggest leap of my life, looking into his brown eyes. "I'm yours," I say. "Make me yours." He growls, bending his knees, his hands go to my hips. In a blink of an eye, my back is against the cold door, and his mouth is on mine. When his tongue meets mine, I think I actually sigh. My hands go to his hips while he attacks my mouth. There is no mistaking this kiss; it's all I want and need. I've never been kissed like this. In all my life, I've never imagined that a kiss could be like this. That one kiss could rock your whole world and make you lose control.

His hands go to my waist as he grips my shirt in his fists. My own hands move to his shirt. Pulling it up, I put my hand on his skin. Every time I've kissed him this week, I've wanted to run my hands all over him. I've wanted to have him on top of me and feel his skin on mine. He moves his head to the left and then to the right, each time trying to deepen the kiss. I rake my nails up his back, and he groans. My mouth swallows his groan as his hand moves up my side and cups my tit. I let go of his mouth to take in the sensation of him. "Baby," he whispers. Attacking my neck, he pushes me harder into the door. His cock presses right on my stomach, and I move on my tippy-toes to have him angle right where I need him to be.

I press into him, and before you know it, he has me picked up, my legs going around his waist. I pull his shirt up. "I want to feel you," I say as he moves to give me access to take his shirt off. I bend down and kiss his chest. I cross my arms and pull my shirt over my head, leaving me with nothing but my black bra. His eyes turn from a deep brown to almost black. "I want to feel your skin on mine," I admit.

"Anything," he says. Bringing his mouth to my neck, he sucks in and bites down just a touch, and the sensation goes through my body all the way to the end of my toes. He comes back to my mouth, my mouth opening for him and my hands go up by my head, my knuckles hitting the door. His mouth leaves mine, and my eyes slowly open to see him go to my neck. I move my head to the side, giving him as much access as he wants. His kisses trail toward my collarbone, and the black bra strap slides down. His tongue comes out as he trails it to the swell of my breast. "Perfection," he says, pushing his hips into me while his hands cup both my tits. "Fucking perfect," he says, pushing the cups down. "And fucking mine." He bends to take a nipple into his mouth. My back arches and my hips move up and down on their own. He moves from the right nipple to the left, biting down and then sucking in. His thumb and index finger rolling the nipple he just left. "Right here," he says, sucking the area right next to my nipple into his mouth. He lets go of it and looks down at the red mark. "Mine."

He wraps his arm around my waist, turning and walking back toward my bedroom. "I want you spread out and open for me," he whispers in my ear right before he puts me down. He squats down in front of me, kissing my stomach while he unties his shirt from around my waist. "I have so many things I'm going to do with these legs." He drags his fingers from my calves all the way up, making me shiver with his touch. "First," he says, his tongue coming out as he licks my stomach, "I want them wrapped around my head." He unbuttons my belt in one motion. "Then I want them …" He unbuttons the button to the jean shorts, and I know they will fall to the floor because they are so big on me. The sound of the zipper joins the sound of my panting. "Around my hips," he says, and the shorts fall to a puddle around my feet. "Fuck," he says, looking at me standing here in my black lace thong. Okay, fine, thong is being generous. It's more of a string with a little triangle.

"When I put these on tonight," I say, and he looks up at me. My hand goes in his hair. "I was hoping that the night would end like this."

His hand goes to the string on the side as his face goes to my pussy. He sucks in, and I can feel the wetness from his mouth meeting my own wetness. I pull his hair, and his hand snaps my thong off. He uses his tongue to lick my slit, and the sound he makes has my knees trembling. It's almost a roar.

"Sit on the bed at the edge and spread your legs for me." He doesn't have to tell me twice. All I have to do is sit and my legs open for him. "Beautiful." He looks up at me. "Every fucking inch of you." He gets between my legs. "Is fucking beautiful." He licks his finger and runs it between my pussy lips, then slips it inside me. My head falls back.

"Too good for me," he mumbles when his hand comes up and opens my pussy to find my clit. The tip of his tongue comes out, and he licks it back and forth while his finger fucks me. "Honey." He licks me up and down, slipping another finger into me. "Tastes like fucking honey." He sucks my clit into his mouth and then bites down on it, and I fall back onto the bed. My eyes close, and he stops moving his fingers. I open my eyes and get up on my elbows.

"Watch me," he says as he licks up again, his hand still holding my lips open for him. "Watch me eat your pussy," he says, and my eyes close for a second while he moves his fingers in faster. "So fucking tight," he says, and my hips move up on their own. "Don't you make me hold you down," he says right before his tongue plays with my clit. "I'm the one who is going to make you come." He sucks in. "And the only one who will make you come." My legs close around his head. "That's my girl," he says, kissing the inside of my thigh softly right before he bites it. "Number two," he says of the mark. "Only a million more to go." He fucks me with his fingers to the edge.

"Asher," I moan, trying to keep my eyes open as I watch him lick and finger fuck me. I feel myself getting tighter and wetter. I shiver when the feeling goes from my clit all the way to the tip of my toes. "I'm almost there."

"I know, baby," he says between licks. "Every fucking day," he says as his fingers move faster. "I'm going to eat this pussy every fucking day." And just like that, I fall over the edge, moaning out his name as my pussy pulsates around his fingers. "I think we can do better than that," he says, moving his fingers so fast the orgasm fades and then comes right back. My elbows give out, and my legs tighten around his head. My eyes close as I see stars. He slowly stops moving, and my heaving chest is covered with a layer of sweat.

Feeling him slip out of me, I open my eyes. He stands, and my legs fall down onto the floor because I have no energy to even hold them up. He's standing between my legs, his own jeans hanging low on his hips. The outline of his cock is very fucking apparent, and I lick my lips. Sitting up, I place my hands on his hips as I kiss his stomach. "What is it you told me?" I ask, my hands moving to the button of his jeans. My hand palms his cock through his jeans and squeezes. He hisses and closes his eyes, and I stop, moving my hands away from him. "You told me to watch." I unbutton his jeans and his zipper starts to go down on its own, giving me a peek at his black boxers. "So you are going to watch." I pull the zipper the rest of the way down. "Watch me suck your cock," I say, pushing his pants and boxers down off his hips. His cock springs free, and I'm the one who groans.

I stand, taking his cock in my hand and moving it up and down. My fingers don't even touch as I move my hand up and down. My hand drops his cock as I kneel on the bed. "Not only are you going to watch me suck your cock." I get onto my hands and knees with my mouth at the right height to slide him into my mouth. "You're going to watch my ass go back and forth while picturing your cock in it." I don't wait for him to answer before I lick the tip of his cock, the pre-cum salty on my tongue. I twirl my tongue around the head of his cock, my hand coming up and jerking him off. I take the head into my mouth and then let it go, each time going down just a touch deeper until I get it in as far as I'm going to go. I move my hand and my mouth at the same speed, his hand coming to move the hair away from my face so he can watch my mouth take his cock. My ass moves from side to side. His hips thrust into my mouth while one of his hands finds my tits, and he plays with my nipple. I let go of his cock, licking down the shaft as my eyes glance up to meet his gaze.

His jaw is tight as I lick and suck one ball into my mouth. "Just decided," he says between clenched teeth when I take his cock into my mouth again. "I'm going to spend all night with my cock in your pussy." It's me who closes my eyes, my stomach getting tight as he plays with my nipple. "You're going to take my cock any way I want to give it to you." I nod my head. "Slow." He has to take a second before he continues. His hips move with the speed of my hand, my spit running down his cock. "Hard." He stops talking. "I'm going to come," he says and tries to take his cock out of my mouth, but my hand pulls him back to me. "I'm coming," he hisses out as my mouth swallows everything he has to give me. I keep going until nothing is left. I get back up on my knees, and his hand goes straight to my pussy, his finger sliding in easily. "Soaked," he says, and I nod. "For me."

"Only you," I say, going over to the bedside table and opening it. I grab the box of condoms I bought two days ago. "I think you have some things planned for me." I open the box of twelve and take one out.

"Oh, I have a lot planned for you," he says, kicking off his shoes and taking his jeans off. I kick my boots off as they join my jean shorts and his jeans. "Get ready, baby." He gets on the bed with me. "It's going to be a long night."

Twenty-Five

Asher

I WATCH HER get on her back in the middle of the bed, and I can't move. This right here is going to be something I'll remember for the rest of my life. If I don't get anything else in this world, this memory will make it all worth it. Bringing the condom wrapper to my mouth, I tear off the top and quickly cover myself.

The whole time she watches me, waiting for me. Her lips are plump from my lips, and her long tanned legs spread, waiting for me. I crawl over her, my mouth going to hers, her tongue coming out hungrily. I fist my cock in my hand and let go of her mouth, rubbing my cock up and down her slit. I can feel the heat through the condom, and I want to just pound into her.

"Asher." She pants my name out, her eyes looking at

my cock. "Now." She moves her hips up to get me into her.

She moves her legs up, wrapping them around my hips to make sure I don't go anywhere. "What do you want, baby?" I ask, and her eyes go to mine.

"You," she says softly. "All of you." I close my eyes to calm myself down, but it doesn't help. In one thrust, I'm balls deep in her. She cries out the same time I do when I realize how fucking snug she is. Her legs tighten even more around my hips. "Again." She eggs me on, and I give it to her. With each thrust, she begs for more, telling me to go harder. I plant myself balls deep in her. Her legs slip from my hips, and my hands go to her thighs, holding her open for me. Her hand comes down to play with herself, and I bend down to take her perky nipple into my mouth. I bite it and suck it into my mouth. Her hips fly up. "Again."

I put my hands on either side of her arms, propping her legs over my shoulders. I turn to kiss her ankle, biting it and seeing my mark on her. I thrust out of her and then back in again. Her finger goes nuts over her clit, and I can tell she's close because I can barely move my cock in her anymore. I watch her eyes as I fuck her, the sound of slapping skin and pants filling the room. Her eyes go from a light blue to a deeper blue, like the deep ends of the ocean, and I can get lost in those eyes every second of every day for the rest of my life. She closes her eyes and arches her back off the bed, and with my name on her lips, she lets go and comes all over my cock. I can't even stop to enjoy it because I'm following her right off the edge. My cock buried deep in her, and with her name in a roar, I let myself go.

Her legs slowly slip off my shoulders, and I slowly fall onto her gently, burying my face in her neck as she wraps her arms and legs around me. I turn to my side, taking her with me, and her hand plays in my hair at the nape of my neck. "I can't move," I admit. My cock is still buried in her.

"Then don't," she says softly. "I like you here." I look up at her, and she kisses my nose. "I like you here a lot," she says. I wait a couple of minutes before I get off the bed, taking her with me. I wrap one hand around her waist, and she locks her legs behind me. "Where are we going?"

"Shower," I tell her, walking into the bathroom. Twenty minutes later, I'm getting out of the shower, dripping water everywhere as I run back into her bedroom to get a condom. Twenty-five minutes after that, I'm setting her on her bathroom counter, and I'm fucking her for the third time in an hour.

She leaves the bathroom before me, and when I walk out, she is under her covers. I stand here wondering if I should go to my room or join her. Her eyes open when she must feel me staring at her. "What are you doing?" She gets up on her elbow.

"I was going to go to bed," I say, and she tilts her head to the side.

"Well, then get into bed." She moves over, leaving me the open spot for me to get into bed. When I pull back the cover and see her naked, my cock twitches. I can't get enough of her.

I get into bed with her, my hand coming out and pulling her to me. She throws her leg over my hip, tilting her head up to kiss my neck. "You don't have any marks on you." She rubs her nose on my jaw. "And I have ten." I laugh. She had three when she got into the shower, and then she had six when she got out, and then she got four more on the counter.

"Where would you put it?" I ask. "Keep in mind that I take off my shirt during the day when I'm working with your family," I remind her, and she groans.

"Buzzkill," she says, making me laugh even more. My mouth touches hers, and we kiss, her tongue coming out to play with mine. It's only a matter of time before I'm sliding into her again. When I finally close my eyes, the sun is coming out.

I hear a phone ringing, and when I open my eyes, all I see is blond hair. "I'm breaking that phone," she says from on top of me. Her head is on my shoulder, her legs thrown over my hips, and her arm is wrapped around my waist. I couldn't move even if I wanted to. "Why is it still ringing?" she groans.

"I can't move and get to my phone," I say, and she leans over the bed, grabbing the phone out of my jeans and turning off the alarm and then tossing it on the side table.

"If it goes off again, I'm running it over with my truck," she says, getting back onto my chest and the position she was in when she woke up. I laugh. "It's not funny."

"We have to get up," I say, turning her to the side and kissing her neck softly. "It's after eleven."

"We just went to bed," she moans when I take a nipple into my mouth, and I don't know if it's because I'm waking her up or she's happy with my mouth. "I need sleep," she says, rolling onto her back.

"You sleep," I say. "I'm going to eat some breakfast." I kiss down her body until I find her pussy. My girl lights up, and when we walk out of the house an hour later, her hand is in mine.

"How are we going to explain this?" Amelia asks. "I can't even walk properly, and my whole body hurts."

"We can say you fell," I say, and she laughs.

"On your dick?" I open the truck door for her, and she gets in and winces. I close the door, laughing to myself, and when I walk around the truck and get in, she leans over and kisses me. "This is going to be a challenge."

"What is?" I ask, pulling away from her house.

"Being in front of my family and not being able to just kiss you or hold your hand," she says, and I look over at her.

"Or we can tell your family?" I wink at her, and she rolls her eyes.

"You know how they are." She turns her back toward the car door. "They'll be all up in our business, and for now, I want it to be just the two of us. I want it to be ours." Her voice trails off.

I grab her hand and bring it to my lips, smiling. "Three hours," I say, looking over and seeing that it's noon. "Make that two."

"I'll fake sick." She looks over at me, and I park my truck on the street. I look around, making sure no one is out or can see before I grab her face and kiss her one last time before we get out of the truck.

She walks slowly beside me, our hands grazing when we walk into the backyard. Ethan is the first one who sees us. "What happened to you?" He looks over at Amelia.

"I was getting a bowl on the top shelf in the kitchen and fell on my ass," she says without skipping a beat.

"Where were you?" He looks over at me, and my tongue gets bigger in my mouth.

"What the hell kind of question is that?" Amelia says, pushing his shoulder. "I don't need a man to help me get a bowl."

"Obviously you do?" He points at her. "You should go see Grandma. I'm sure she has some home remedy in that book of hers." He takes a look around before he tells her the next part. "Yeah." He turns, looking out at the crowd of people who are there. "Reed showed up with Hazel today."

"Hazel who?" She turns and tries to find him in the crowd. "Dammit. She's one of my best waitresses," she hisses. "He needs to stop dating my staff members."

Amelia looks at me and then back at Ethan before walking away, and I have to roll my lips when I see her put her hand on her back. "I feel bad for the guy who has to deal with her," he says, and I can't look him in the eye. I feel like I've lied to him.

"He'll be fine," I mumble out. "I'm going to go and get some food," I say. "You coming with?"

"Nah," he says. "We ate already."

"Okay," I say, looking around to see if I can spot Amelia. She looks over at the same time as I spot her, and I motion with my head toward the food. She nods and walks to me, and I try not to laugh.

"Hey," I say when she gets close enough, and I can't stop the smile on my face. My hand itches to grab her face and kiss her.

"There you are." I hear over my shoulder and turn to see Billy coming toward us. "I was wondering where you were," he says. He slaps me on my shoulder, smiling, and then going to Amelia. Her eyes light up when she smiles at him. "You look tired."

"I didn't get much sleep last night," she tells him, and I look down at the grass as the gnawing guilt hits me.

"Go get something to eat and get back home," he tells her, then turns to look at me. "You make sure you take her right to bed." He slaps my arm. "See you tomorrow."

"Well, you heard the man." She smirks at me. "You better make sure you take me straight to bed."

I laugh, shaking my head. "I couldn't even look him in the eye," I admit. "I thought for sure he would know that I saw you naked." She puts her head back and laughs. "It's not funny. Even with Ethan, I couldn't even look at him."

"Your secret is safe with me." She steps closer and looks up at me, and if we were anywhere else, I would kiss her. Instead, all I can do is look into her eyes and smile, hoping she knows just how bad I want her.

"Good to know," I say softly. "Now, let's grab

something to eat, and let's get you home to bed."

"Yes, please," she says, turning and walking toward the table of food. I watch her go and then feel eyes on me. I look around, seeing everyone doing their own thing and no one really looking at me. I ignore the uneasy feeling that I get, telling myself it's only because of the guilt I feel in my gut for lying not only to her family but also to her.

Twenty-Six

AMELIA

I FEEL HIM kiss my shoulder and then slide out of bed. I open one eye and watch him, my heart skipping a beat when I do. Everything, and I mean everything, about him is perfect. He grabs a pair of shorts from the laundry basket that sits in the corner of the room and puts them on. "Why are you putting on clothes?" I try to get up, but my body feels like it just did a five-hour workout.

"I'm going to get you coffee." He looks over at me, and I see my mark on his chest. "Because we have to get going." He comes back over and kisses the same shoulder I felt him kiss before.

I turn over onto my back and look out the window at the sun straining to come in through the curtains. I look over and see that it's past ten o'clock. My eyes close again for a second and then I smell the coffee coming from the kitchen. It's become our morning routine, him getting up and making me coffee.

It's been one week since I asked him to take me to bed. It's been one week that I've woken up every single day with him holding me, kissing me, touching me, wanting me. Last night at the bar, I almost slipped and leaned in to kiss him when he made me laugh at something. I caught myself right before I got on my tippy-toes.

It was shocking to be so open with touching him. I touch him all the time, even in public, and not once did he step away from me. Not once did he look around him to make sure no one was watching.

"Here you go," he says, coming in with two coffee cups in his hands. I sit up, holding the blanket on my chest as I grab the cup of coffee. He gets in bed with me, sitting on his side. "Do you want to shower together?" he asks, and I look over at him.

"For the last seven days," I say, taking a sip of coffee. "Every single time I've joined you in the shower, we've been late."

He smiles, bringing his own cup of coffee to his lips. "And it's always fun." He winks at me, and I laugh, leaning over and kissing his lips.

"That it is," I say, softly kissing his lips again. "That it always is."

"You tired?" He gets up out of bed and puts the cup on the bedside table next to his phone and wallet.

Looking around the room, I spot the little things that remind me of him. His clothes from last night on the floor along with mine. His clothes in the same basket mine are in, a little cup of fresh lavender that he picked up one day from the field and brought back for me.

He comes over to my side of the bed and holds out his hand. I give him the empty cup, and he puts it beside him on the nightstand. His hand comes back, his palm out. "Let's go," he says, and I put my hand in his.

"Where are we going?" I ask, my heart pounding because I think I would go anywhere with him.

"Shower," he says, putting his hands on the sides of my neck. "It's not good without you." He kisses me and then grabs my hand, pulling me with him to the shower. We spend way too much time in there, and when I get out, I have to rush to get dressed.

"Okay," I say, coming out of the walk-in closet to see him making the bed. "I'm ready." I look over at him, and he has black jeans on with a white shirt. It's an outfit I've seen more than once, yet today, he looks extra hot in it.

"Take that look off your face." He points at me, and I just look at him. "You had that same look in your eyes on Thursday night when we closed the bar."

I put my hands on my hips and roll my eyes. "I didn't see you objecting when I got down on my knees." I walk to him and kiss his neck. "Nor did you object when I bent over." I tap his stomach. "Now, let's go before I get back on my knees."

I go to walk out of the room but then look over my shoulder at him. He adjusts his cock that is starting to show exactly what he wants me to do. "Are we going?"

"Oh, we're going," he says, walking to me. "But

just so you know, when we get home later, I'm going to fuck that sass out of you." He slaps my ass, walking to the door. How did I go from having the upper hand to begging him to fuck the sass out of me? He waits for me at the front door, only turning the handle when I get close to him.

I walk out, and he joins me, his hand sliding into mine as we walk to the truck. I get in, ignoring the flip that my stomach just did. He kisses me right before he closes the door, and the whole way to my grandparents', he sits with my hand in his on his leg.

We get there with everyone else, so I can't give him one more kiss before getting out of the truck. He turns off the truck and looks over at me. "Ready?"

I nod my head and get out of the truck to see Gabriel running over to me. "Auntie Amelia, I lost a tooth, and the tooth fairy came." He shows me his bottom teeth, the middle one missing.

"How much did he bring?" I ask, putting my hands around his shoulders as I walk to my brother and Emily.

"Fifty dollars," he says, jumping up and down. I look over at my brother, shocked.

"Fifty dollars," I repeat. "I need to speak to the tooth fairy that used to come to my house." I look at Ethan. "Once I got an IOU paper."

"Go and tell Grandma and Grandpa," I tell Gabriel. "The tooth fairy might have stopped here also." He looks at me, shocked, and then all you can see is his hair flying in the wind as he runs into the back, calling my grandparents.

"Seriously?" I look over at Ethan.

"He lost his tooth at nine o'clock," he says. "It was that or the hundred."

I try to roll my lips. "The struggle must have been real."

He pushes my shoulder as everyone laughs. The minute we get to the barbecue, I go one way and Asher goes the other. I walk over to my mother who sits by herself and see Gabriel collecting money from my father. "Hi," I say when I get close enough, and she looks at me, and she smiles big.

"Hey, baby girl," she says. "He's going to walk out of this backyard a very rich boy," she says, pointing at Gabriel, who is getting money from my uncle Casey. I pull out the empty chair right beside her and sit down. "Do you want some lemonade?" my mother asks, and I just shake my head. "Are you okay?"

"I'm fine, why?" I ask, and she smiles and then looks down at the table, then up at me again.

"You're just …" she says. "You're just different."

My eyebrows pinch together in confusion. "How so?" I ask.

"One, you look happier," she says. "And two, your eyes shine all the time."

"My eyes are the same they have always been."

"No, they aren't," she says, and I can see her eyes filling with tears. "There was a sadness in them." She blinks away the tears.

"There was no sadness there." My stomach sinks.

"There was," she tells me. "And you can deny it and

ignore it, but it was there and now ..." Her hand comes up to cup my cheek. "But now there is a light in them that I've never seen." Her eyes leave mine and go into the direction of Asher, who stands there talking and laughing with my father and Ethan. "He's good for you," she says.

I swallow the lump in my throat. "It's nothing," I finally say, the words coming out in a whisper.

"It's not nothing." She puts her hand on mine. "It's everything." She is about to say something else when my aunt Olivia calls her inside. She gets up, rubbing my head. "Don't push it away."

I sit in the chair for what feels like an eternity. Only moving to get food and then when Asher comes to get me to leave.

I get into the truck, the whole time not saying anything. He reaches out and grabs my hand once he gets into the car and kisses the top of my hand once we drive away from my grandparents' house. "Are you okay?" he asks when he pulls into the driveway of my house.

My hand reaches to open the door. "Yeah, I'm just tired, I guess." I get out of the truck, and for the first time, I don't attack him when we get into the door. Instead, I walk over to the kitchen and open the fridge to get a water bottle out.

"What's wrong?" He stands there in the middle of the living room, looking at me. "You can't tell me you're just tired. I've seen your tired face before." His hand goes up and points at me. "Something happened today at the barbecue, and I'm not going to drop it until you tell me."

I look down, gathering all the courage I need for this next part. Knowing that in one small move, he can shatter me. "My mother said I looked different." His eyebrows pinch together in the same confused face I must have given my mother. "I fell in love without even knowing it." The lump starts to grow bigger in my throat. Heat rushes up my back to my neck, and I think I'm going to be physically sick. "I fell in love, and I didn't even know it was happening until it did." I blink away the tears. "I'm in love with you," I say the words while my heart soars in my chest. "And I know without a shadow of a doubt that I won't survive without you." I wipe the lone tear that comes out of the corner of my eye.

"I don't know what love is," he finally says. "Never knew love growing up, never knew love when I became a man." He walks to me and turns me to look at him. "What I do know is that being with you makes breathing easier. I know that when you walk into a room, all I can do is smile. I know that kissing you is the single best thing I'll ever do in my life. I know that the thought of being without you makes my chest hurt. A pain that feels like something is pressing or stomping on my body and crushing my bones." He pushes the hair away from my face, his big hands coming up to cup my face, and right before his lips meet mine, he says the words that I've never heard from anyone but my family. "I love you, Amelia."

Twenty-Seven

Asher

"WHAT TIME ARE you going to be done?" I ask Amelia when I walk into her office at the barn. She looks up at me, and again, for the I don't know how many times, I stop and smile at her. Leaning back in her chair, she folds her hands on her stomach.

"I'm done at three," she says. "Like I am every single day. So in three hours." I walk over to her desk and sit on the side of it. It's the closest I can get to her without touching her. It's something I often do, and if someone came in, it wouldn't look out of sorts.

"Did you eat lunch?" she asks, and I smirk at her, looking around to make sure no one is lingering or can hear me. My voice goes low anyway.

"I can tell you what I want to eat for lunch." I wink at

her, and she shakes her head.

"You had that for breakfast." She laughs.

"Well, I'll be having that for dinner also." I get up, standing by her chair. "Just so you know."

I want to bend down and kiss her lips, but I know it's not the time.

It's been over a month since I told her I loved her. A month that I've had to hide it, and if I'm honest, I am about done with it. But before I tell everyone about us, I have to come clean to Ethan and Jacob. "I'll see you later." I smile at her, and she tilts her head back, and I glare at her. "Why do you tempt me like this?"

"Because I want a kiss," she says, and I walk to her door and close it.

Standing in front of it, I call her over. "Come here."

She walks to me and her arms go around my shoulders. "We need to think about what we should tell people." I look into her eyes as my nose rubs hers. "I think it's time."

"Me, too." She smiles and kisses my lips.

"I have to talk to your father and Ethan first." I push away the hair from her face, knowing that after I talk to them, I have to come clean to her. "Then we can do that." My heart picks up, wondering how she will take the truth. I kiss her one last time. "Okay, I have to head over to help your grandfather." Her hands fall from my neck. "He has someone coming to pick up something." I sneak in one more kiss before I open the door and walk out to my truck.

I take my phone out before I chicken out and send

Jacob and Ethan a group text.

Me: Was wondering if I could talk to you two tonight.

I put the phone in my pocket as I make my way over to Billy's barn. When I pull in, there is already a brand-new pickup parked in the lane. I get out and walk toward the barn, seeing Billy with his hands on his hips. He listens to what the guy in front of him is saying, and even though he's smiling, I know that it's not a real smile. I walk to them, and the man turns to look at me. "If there is anyone who knows, it's this guy," Billy says. The man turns and holds out his hand.

"Nice to meet you," the man says. "I'm Tex."

"Asher," I say my name, taking his hand and then looking at Billy to see how he responds to this guy. His eyes never leave the man. "What can I do for you?"

"My hay shipment is running late," he says. "Was wondering if I could maybe borrow some to hold off."

"I think we should be okay," I say, then turn to look at Billy, who just nods his head. "I can get you a couple, and you can send over some guys after to get more."

"Sounds good," he says, and I turn to walk into the barn going to where he keeps his hay.

"Thank you," Tex says from beside me when we walk into the barn. "I wasn't sure Billy was going to go for it," he says, and my whole body becomes tight. "I used to work here," he says. "And I left him without notice." He continues talking when he stops right in front of the hay. "I actually had your job," he says, smirking.

"Really?" I ask. "I've never heard your name before." I grab the gloves out of my pocket.

"Doesn't surprise me," he says, standing in front of me. "I broke his granddaughter's heart," he says, smiling slyly while my whole body becomes a block of ice.

"I'll grab one, and you grab the other." I ignore him and walk over, grabbing the ties of the hay and walking out to his truck. He follows me, and I wait for him to walk ahead of me, opening the bed of his truck. I slide my bale of hay into his truck and then stand back while he does his. Taking off my gloves, I put them back in my back pocket. He closes the back hatch and then looks at me.

"Thanks for your help," he says, reaching in his back pocket and taking something out. He holds out his hand with a white business card between two fingers. "If you're ever looking for work."

My hand comes out and grabs the card and I look down at it. His name is in bold black letters, and I want to laugh. "I believe I owe you a thank-you." I flip the card. "Oh," I say, putting the card in my pocket and then coming back, swinging a punch. I hit him square in the jaw, and he stumbles back. "That's for Amelia." His eyes go big. "Get the fuck out of here before I tell Billy why you really left."

He stands, the corner of his lip bleeding. "And just so we're clear. Don't come back here because we aren't into helping assholes." I turn back and walk back to the barn, stopping midway when I see Billy leaning against the door of the barn.

The sound of a truck door slamming and then the sound of the crushing of rocks makes my body relax.

"Um," I say, and I don't even know what I'm going to say or how I can explain this. "He's not coming back." I look down at my hand, squeezing it into a fist. "I'll cover the cost of those two."

Billy looks at me and laughs. "I believe I owe you," Billy says. "One for that scene." He points to the place where I decked Tex. "And two for what you've done for Amelia."

"I haven't done anything," I say, the guilt working its way through me. I can't even look at him in the eye.

"I'm glad." He walks to me and slaps my shoulder. "I don't know what happened between her and Tex," he says. "And from the way she was after he left, I don't want to know or else that punch that he just got will be the least of his injuries. Now go get some ice on that hand." He walks away laughing and shaking his head.

I go back to the barn to see Amelia, first stopping by the freezer to get some ice in a bag and wrap it around my knuckles. I walk into her office, and she is on the phone, her head coming up as she sees me. Her eyes go from mine to my hand, then back up again to look at my face. "I'm going to get back to you." She hangs up the phone and gets up. Her face fills with worry. "What happened?"

"I met Tex," I say, and her face goes white. "Yeah, so …"

"Where?" she asks, walking around the desk.

"The barn. He was there to borrow some hay, and well, I put two and two together," I say. "When he left, he handed me his business card, and I decked him."

"You hit him?" she asks, shocked.

241

"I did thank him first," I say, and she picks up my hand. "Then I hit him."

She drops my hand and walks out of her office, calling Willow. "Can you take my place in the office for the rest of the day?" she asks, and Willow comes out of a stall.

"Of course," Willow says. Looking at her and then me, she drops her eyes to my hand. "Is everything okay?"

"Yup," Amelia says. "Just going to go home and make sure his hand is okay, and then I'm going to eat lunch." Willow nods at her and tries to hide a smile. "I'll drive," Amelia says, walking out to the truck, and I just nod awkwardly at Willow.

"Have a good lunch," she says, laughing and turning to walk into the office.

I get into the truck and look over at Amelia. "What did I miss?" I ask, and she smiles at me.

"I'm going to thank you." She puts the truck in drive. "One for hitting the asshole and two for being you," she says, making her way over to her house, and thank me she does.

When I drop her off at the bar, it's almost four o'clock, and I make my way over to Jacob's house. I park the car, seeing Ethan sitting outside with him as the two of them talk. I get out of the truck, and my whole body starts to shake. Shakes with news, shakes with anticipation, shakes with the fear that they might not accept me. "Hey," I say, walking up the driveway toward them.

"There he is," Ethan says. "Rocky." I look at him. "Word on the street is you laced good old Tex."

"Yeah." I put my hands in my back pockets. "Guy

rubbed me the wrong way."

"Is that so?" Jacob says, looking at me.

"I was wondering if I could speak to the two of you," I say, my mouth getting so dry I don't even attempt to swallow.

"I think we know what you want to tell us," Ethan says, laughing, and I look at him. "You have a thing for Amelia."

"What?" I ask, shocked.

"We know," Jacob says. "I know she is my daughter, and I love her with everything that I have, but that woman can push anyone to their limits." He shakes his head. "So if you're still living with her after all this time"—he holds out his hand—"you have to like her at the very least."

"Does that mean you're staying?" Ethan asks. "We both thought you were coming here to tell us that you're staying."

"Um," I say, shocked with so many things going through my head. "There is also something you guys need to know."

Ethan looks at me, and he can sense from my tone that it has nothing to do with Amelia. "I should have told you when I first came to town," I say and then stop talking when Jacob's phone rings. He takes it out of his pocket and answers it.

"Hey, baby girl," he says, and then his face drops. "Truck," he says to us, and I'm already running to my truck. My heart's in my chest, thinking that Tex went to pay her a visit. Jacob gets into the truck passenger seat, and I watch for Ethan to close the door in the back before I take off. "Lock the door," he tells her. "Don't let anyone in until I get there."

Twenty-Eight

AMELIA

Thirty minutes earlier

"I'LL SEE YOU soon." I lean over the truck and kiss his lips. "Try not to get into any more fights."

He rolls his eyes, shaking his head. "It was one fight," he says, "and I'd do it all over again." My heart speeds up when he says that. When he showed up at the barn, I could tell from the look on his face that something just happened. Then I saw the ice around his hand, and my heart sank. The minute he said Tex's name, I knew this was going downhill. What I didn't know is that instead, it soared higher than I've ever been. I have never felt so loved in my life than I was at that moment. For someone to fight for me was everything.

I get out of the truck and walk in, turning off the alarm as the phone in my purse rings. I grab it as I walk to the back office. Chelsea's name flashes on the screen with a picture of the two of us taken three weeks ago. "Hello," I say, pressing my shoulder up to hold it to my ear.

"Hello," she says. "Is that all you have to say to me is hello?" I can hear that she is in her car on Bluetooth.

"What else does one say when answering their phone?" I laugh, walking into the office. I dump my purse into the chair and pick up the mail on the floor. The mail that fell on the floor yesterday after he bent me over this desk. I smile, thinking about him.

"So I heard a rumor today," Chelsea says.

"Really?" I say, putting the mail on the desk, then turning and walking out of the office. "And what is this rumor that you heard?"

"That you are knocking boots with Asher," she says, laughing, and I stop walking when she says this. "I wish I was there right now to see the expression on your face."

"There is no expression on my face," I lie to her, and she just laughs even harder, making me shake my head.

"I knew it," she says. "I knew it, and everyone told me I was silly."

"You are silly," I confirm.

"Okay, did you or did you not take him home today to have nasty-ass sex because he beat up that sorry excuse for a human Tex?" she asks, and I walk behind the bar. "Your silence is a yes."

"My silence is because I'm shocked that my family are gossip queens," I say, and then I close my eyes. "Who is saying these things?" I ask softly.

"Well, Willow called me, and I called Emily," she starts, and I groan. "If you don't make a statement, the aunts are going to be calling each other, and then you'll be pregnant by the end of the night."

I laugh because she is not wrong. "Fine," I admit. "I'm with Asher."

"Oh, please," she says, and I can feel her rolling her eyes. "Tell me something I don't know."

"What do you want to know?" I ask.

"How long?" she asks, and my head hangs.

"Over a month," I say, and she gasps out in shock.

"What?" she asks. "How is it that no one saw it?"

"You just told me that you knew about it," I remind her.

"Yeah, we figured it out this weekend when someone saw him slap your ass behind the bar and you didn't throat punch him," she says, laughing.

"Well, you know," I say, turning when I hear a car door slam. "And I'm not with child either, so when you call your mother after this phone call, you can let her know."

"How do you know I'm going to call my mother after this phone call?" she asks, and it's me who laughs.

"This is the juiciest information that you have at the moment," I say. "And I know you will be dying to tell everyone that I confirmed it."

"Well, there is one person I'm not telling," she says. "You need to do that yourself."

"I'm going to call him tomorrow," I say and then hear

the front door open. "I got to go. Talk to you later." I hang up the phone, looking at the door.

The man comes in wearing a tan suit, and I know right away he isn't from here. "Sorry, we're closed," I say, and he takes off his aviator glasses that he's wearing, looks around, and then looks at me smiling.

"This place sure has changed," he says, walking in a bit, his black hair falling on his forehead. I watch him walk to the bar. "I used to come here when I was in school." He smiles at me. "Thought I would swing by before I left town again."

He sits on the stool right in front of me, and something about the way he looks at me makes my skin crawl. "I'm sorry, I didn't get your name." I pretend that I'm not bothered by him.

He laughs, putting his hands on the bar and tapping his finger. "You are just like your mother."

"You know my mother?" I ask, and he smirks.

"We are somewhat related," he says, and I tilt my head.

"I'm sorry, I don't know who you are?" I tell him, my heart sinking, and I wish I had a button that I could press to call someone. "But if you like, I can tell my mother and father that you stopped by." I pick up my phone and look at him.

He smirks at me, getting up. "Oh, you tell her, sugar," he says, and everything in me is telling me to run. "Tell them Liam stopped by." The minute he says his name, I know I'm in trouble. "Also, tell my boys I'll be in touch," he says, turning and walking out.

The phone in my hand shakes as I call my father, who answers right away. "Hey, baby girl," he says, and I feel somewhat okay knowing I'm on the phone with him. Knowing that no matter what, he is going to make sure I'm safe.

"Dad," I say, my voice filled with fear. "Liam was just here."

"Truck!" he yells. "Lock the door," he says. I rush over to the door and lock it, looking out the window. "Don't let anyone in until I get there."

"He's gone," I say, my heart beating in my chest as I turn and slide down to the floor. "Should I leave?"

"Hey." I hear Asher's voice come onto the phone, and I sob out. "I'm there in two minutes, you hear me." I nod my head, my whole body shaking. "I need to hear your voice."

I hear the sound of rocks flying, and I get up looking out the window, seeing my uncle Beau flying out of his car, not even closing the door. "Uncle Beau is here," I say, dropping my phone and opening the door. "Uncle Beau," I say, and I fly into his arms.

"I'm here," he says. "You're okay." He rubs my head. "I'm here."

I hear the stop of a truck, and the door flies open, and Asher runs in. His eyes are on Beau and then me. "Are you okay?" he asks, and I nod.

My father and brother are the next ones in, followed by Casey and Quinn. "I have the feed," Casey says, walking in. "He looks just as slimy as he did back then."

Then he looks at Beau. "Sorry."

Beau walks over to the phone in Casey's hand as the guys watch the feed, and I feel Asher take me into his arm. "You okay?"

"Yeah," I say, looking up at him. "I'm okay."

"What the fuck is he doing here?" Ethan says, and I just look at him. "Like why come here for what?"

"I have no idea," Beau says. "Last I heard, he was signing his third divorce and had alimony payments up the ass." He looks at his phone.

My father comes over to me. "Did he say anything to you?"

I nod my head. "He said he used to come here back when he was growing up." I start to tell them. "He said he knew you and Mom. Then he said tell my boys I'll be in touch."

"What the actual fuck?" Ethan says, and we all look at him. "What the fuck does that mean?"

My uncle Beau takes his phone out of his pocket. "I'm going to call him right now, and I'll fucking kick his ass myself."

"It makes no sense," my father says. "No fucking sense."

"If he gets close to Gabriel or me," Ethan says, his voice so tight and so vicious. "I'll fucking kill him with my bare hands." Something about his tone I know he isn't kidding.

"He isn't looking for you guys," Asher says from beside me, and all eyes are on his. His body goes tight right beside me. I look over at him, and I can see the anguish all over his face.

"What the fuck are you talking about right now?" Quinn says, his stance ready to attack Asher.

"He's looking for me," Asher says from beside me, and for the second time in my life, my world crashes. "I'm his son."

Twenty-Nine

ASHER

"HE'S LOOKING FOR me." The words come out in almost a whisper. "I'm his son," I finally say out loud and feel Amelia get stiff beside me. I want to take her in the back and talk to her one on one, but the eyes looking at me tell me this is not an option. Not with everyone's eyes on me. "I'm his son." I repeat the words again in case I didn't say them clear enough before.

"I'm sorry, what did you say?" Ethan steps forward, confusion all over his face as his eyes meet mine.

"This isn't how I wanted to do this." I look at him and then Jacob, who stands there with shock and confusion all over his face. He just stares at me, and I know I have one chance to say this. I just hope that in the end, they don't toss me out on my ass. I also know that in the end,

I'll deserve it for lying to them. "You have to know that none of this was supposed to happen." I can feel Amelia pull away from me like the wick at the end of a candle burning out. She moves slowly, and I watch her walk over to stand by Jacob. My hand is stuck to my side instead of reaching out and holding her next to me. The tears in her eyes are forming, shattering my soul.

"Why don't you start at the beginning?" Jacob says and puts his arm around Amelia. He brings her closer to him, rubbing his thumb up and down her arm. The same arm that held me earlier today, the same arm that I kissed not too long ago. It kills me because that is supposed to be my job. I'm supposed to be the one holding her when she needs it. I'm the one who is supposed to be drying her tears, not making her cry. I'm the one she should turn to, not the one she runs away from.

"I need." Beau holds up his hand, stopping me from saying anything else. He moves past me, going behind the bar. He grabs the whiskey on the top shelf and a shot glass. Everyone looks over at him. "Anyone else need one?" He holds up the bottle, no one moving toward him. "No, just me?" He pours himself a shot and then takes it. He hisses out and pours himself another one, this time no hissing coming out of him. "I think I'm good." He pours another one but leaves it in front of him. "But just in case, I'm going to stay here."

I look back over, my eyes trying to get Amelia to look at me. I'm silently screaming at her to look in my direction. Her head is bent, and her eyes are focused on her hands wringing in front of her. A lone teardrop falls on her hands, and she shakes it away as if she was being burned by fire. "I never knew who my father was." I start the story, looking at every single man who stands in this bar. These men who have taken me under their wing and embraced me. "When I turned eighteen, I went and got a copy of my birth certificate, hoping by some miracle she would have put a name down. But it was blank." I laugh bitterly that this is my fucking life. "It was father unknown." My eyes fly to Amelia who looks anywhere but at me. "I don't know why I was surprised by it. It wasn't like I was going to go search for him or anything like that. It was just a hope that maybe, just maybe I would have someone out there."

"I feel a huge but coming on," Ethan says, looking at me, and then Beau groans and takes another shot.

"I was working at the grill in this tiny shithole of a restaurant." I shake my head. "I was making under minimum wage, but I had no choice. It was in the middle of fucking bum fuck when the door opens. I looked up because the bell usually didn't ring that often. A man steps in wearing a three-piece suit. I laughed, thinking this guy was for sure lost. He looked around and spotted me right away. Pointing at me, he asked if my name was Asher." I swallow the lump in my throat. "He asked me who my mother was, and at first, I was confused, and then I thought this could be my father."

"It wasn't," Beau says right away. "In order for him to be a father at all to you, he would have to acknowledge you, and from our experience, he doesn't give a shit where he leaves his fucking seed." He takes another shot and then looks at Ethan. "I love you with everything I have, and you know that." Ethan just nods at him.

"It wasn't Liam," I confirm to him. "I also didn't tell this man who my mother was. I didn't answer anything. He held out a manila envelope," I say, and Ethan gasps out.

"No," he says, shaking his head, and he walks over to the bar to stand next to Beau who just hands him the bottle. He doesn't even bother grabbing a shot glass. Instead, he drinks straight from the bottle. His hand is shaking when he puts the bottle down on the bar. "How old were you?" Ethan asks me.

"I had just turned," I say, and Ethan finishes with me, "Twenty-one."

"How the fuck do you know?" I look at him, shocked he knew this. No one knew this because I didn't tell a soul. One because I had no one to tell, and two because no one would believe me.

"Did the man tell you that it was your truth?" Ethan says, and it's my turn to need a drink. But my feet don't move from my spot. He must see from my face that he is hitting it right on the spot. The back of my neck burns as my stomach sinks even more to the floor. "How old are you?" he asks.

"Going to be thirty in a month," I say, and he shakes his head and laughs, but the laughter is soon followed by the bottle in his hand.

"Four months," Ethan says. "I'm younger than you by four months."

"What was in the envelope?" Jacob says. "We need to

know what was in that envelope."

"What wasn't in that fucking envelope," I say, and I hear sniffling from Amelia, who looks at her father.

"A letter from Clint Huntington," I say, and I hear Beau hiss out from behind the bar.

He shakes his head. "That would be dear old grandpa to you." He claps his hands together. "Even from his grave, the fucker is getting his jollies."

"It had the name of a paternity test that was taken a day after I was born," I tell them, "with the results stating that Liam Huntington was my father." I shake my head. "I had a name. For the first time in my life, I had a name. It took me a month to get the courage to go and look him up online. I went to one of those libraries and typed in his name. His wedding photo was the first thing to come up and then you," I say, pointing at Beau. "All about how you were mayor of this town." I shrug. "For the first time in my life, I had a family. I had someone who was a part of me. It was as if I won the jackpot."

"It's been nine years," Ethan says. "It took you nine years to come here?"

"I wanted to be sure of myself before I just came here and told you who I was," I tell him. "I still wasn't sure what was going on. Was this letter even real, or was it a joke? I came to town intending to find out who you were," I answer them honestly. "I didn't know anything else besides who Beau was," I tell Ethan. "I was on my way out of town when we met at the diner. I thought for sure you would see that I was hiding something. I thought for sure I would wake up one day, and you guys would have figured it out."

"I can't," she says. I take one step forward, and she looks up at me, stopping me. The look of hatred fills her face, and it cuts me off at my knees.

Quinn steps forward. "I'll take her," he says to Jacob, who just nods at him. He puts his arm around her and turns her, walking out the door.

"I have to," I say, and Jacob and Casey both shake their heads at me.

"You need to give her space," they tell me, and I just look at them.

"Fuck the space," I say, angry. "I was going to tell you guys tonight. It's why I texted you. I was so fucking over this cloud hanging over me. I was so fucking fed up with keeping this fucking secret. I thought if you guys knew who I was and if you got to know me, it wouldn't matter who the fuck my father was."

"He is not your father," Jacob says. "No matter what you have to say, that man is not your father." I blink away the tears in my eyes. "You share DNA with him. That's it." I try to swallow, but nothing goes down, my mouth is dry again. "The question is, what does he want from you?" He looks at me, then at Ethan. "What does he want from either of you?"

"He doesn't want shit from me because he knows if he looks my way, I'll put a bullet up his ass," Ethan says, looking at Beau. "When was the last time he reached out to you?"

"The envelope," Casey says. "Where is this envelope?"

"I have it in a safety-deposit box two towns over," I

say. "Why?"

"The barn you lived in," Casey tells me, and everything around me starts to turn. "You lived in the barn, and it goes up in flames."

"Then you live with Amelia, and she gets knocked over the head," Ethan says, looking at his father.

"Then your car is ransacked along with Amelia's," Jacob says. "All this time, he's been out for you."

"I didn't even know he existed, and I doubted that he gave me a second thought," I tell them.

"The pieces are all here," Casey says, his hand going in a circle. "We just have to put it together."

"Great," Beau says. "Another fucking puzzle."

"We need to see the envelope," Casey says, and I nod at him.

"I can go get it tomorrow," I say to him.

"I'll come with you," Jacob says. "We don't know if he's waiting for you or following you."

"I'll come with you also," Ethan says to me. "We'll figure this out."

"I have to go," I tell them, not sure what the fuck will happen tomorrow, but I know that one thing has to happen right now, and that is me going to Amelia. "I can't leave her with her space. It's going to fucking kill her." I look at Jacob. "I was also going to tell you that I'm in love with your daughter."

Ethan laughs, and I turn to look over at him as Beau's head is down, and he laughs silently. "It's the worst-kept secret of life," Casey says.

"Everyone knows," Beau says.

"She won't forgive me for this," I say my fear out loud. "I know she won't, and I have to accept it." The numbness comes to me. "But I have to at least see her."

"Do you have a place to stay tonight?" Jacob asks, and I just look at him.

"Even if I'm not in her house," I say, "I'm not leaving her. I'll sleep in the truck in front of her house." I swallow down. "And if anyone fucks with her, I'll kill them. I have nothing left to lose. I can spend the rest of my life in jail as long as she's safe," I say, walking out of the bar.

Thirty

Amelia

I DON'T SAY a word as we make our way to my house. "Are you okay?" I hear from Quinn beside me. He walked me out the door, but as soon as the door closed behind him, he picked me up. It didn't help that my knees buckled, and I almost face-planted into the gravel road.

"No," I answer him honestly, staring out at the blue sky. My stomach is a ball of fire. "Not in the slightest," I say, my eyes never leaving the front of the truck.

"Do you want me to call Chelsea?" he asks, and I just shake my head.

"I just need to be alone right now," I say when he pulls up to my house. "My head is just …"

"Will you call me if you need me?" he asks when my hand comes out and grabs the handle of the door. "If not me, then at least someone." I look down, blinking away the tears. "You shouldn't be here alone," he says.

I look back at the house. "Actually …" I swallow down my pride. "Do you think I could stay with you tonight?" I ask him, my bottom lip trembling. "It's totally okay if you have plans."

"Go get your bag," Quinn tells me. "I'll wait for you here." I nod and open the door. "Um," he says, and I look back at him. "You know he's going to show up here." I close my eyes, knowing he is right. "I would hear him out, regardless of what he did."

I hold up my hand, not ready to hear anything that anyone has to say about him. In the end, he lied to me, just like Tex did; the only difference is people actually know about it. The only difference is people will look at me and know the mistakes I've made. "I don't want to."

"Go get your things," he says, and I nod at him, getting out of the truck and allowing the tears to come. Better now, when I'm alone, than in front of everyone. I unlock and open the door, the cold air hitting me, and I can smell him in the air. I close the door behind me softly and head to my bedroom.

I stop at the doorway and look at the room, the bed still a mess from this afternoon. I walk in and smell him all around me. The woodsy smell that only he gives out, the smell that made me feel so fucking safe.

I bend to pick up his T-shirt on the floor beside the bed and bring it to my nose. The sob comes through me when I sit on the bed. I'm shocked and stunned. Never would I have imagined this. Never would I have thought that he would be the one to do this to me. To lie to me.

I look over at the side table, seeing his stuff on there, and my hand goes to my stomach. I look over at the corner of the room where his stuff is on the chair. He's everywhere I look, and I know that I have to get out of here.

I walk to the closet and grab a bag when I hear the front door open and slam shut. My hands shake when I hear the footsteps come closer and closer, the bag dropping on the floor.

I turn to walk out of the closet when I see him standing there at the entrance to the bedroom. I look at him, and my heart shatters in my chest. I was right about one thing. I will not get over him. "Baby," he says, his voice in a whisper, and I shake my head. I hold up my hand, no words coming up over the lump in my throat.

"Don't," I finally muster out. "I don't."

"Listen to me, please," he says, taking a step into the room. My body aches for his touch, wanting him to put his palm on my cheek and his thumb to wipe away the tears that don't stop pouring out.

"There is nothing to say," I say, anger starting to take over. "You're a liar." Three words I never thought I would say to him.

"I never lied to you," he says, his voice tight. "Never."

"Omitting that you were half brothers with Ethan," I say as I step out of my closet, "is the same as fucking lying." I lash out at him.

"What I told you about myself was the truth," he says. "Everything I told you was my truth."

"You used my family and me," I say, and it's his turn to take a step back as if I slapped him across the face. "You came here knowing who you were and who we were." I shrug my shoulders. "I was just a stupid girl who fell in love with you." I shake my head. "Or was that a lie, too? You know, get more into the family before you told us who you really were."

"Nothing," he hisses. "Nothing between us was a lie. I love you, Amelia. I love you with every fucking bone in my body. I love you with every fiber of my being. I love you with every breath I take." I ignore the way my body wants to go to him. I ignore the pull of his words. I ignore it all. "You don't think it killed me every single day waking up next to you having this on my mind."

"Well, obviously not enough to let you tell me the truth." I swallow the pain in my chest, the burning in my stomach starts to grow. The fear of breaking down in front of him, making the back of my neck burn. He doesn't deserve to see you fall, I tell myself. "I did it again," I say, my voice trembling no matter how much I fight it off. The tears come, and I have no more energy left to stop them. All I know is that I have to get out of here before I crumple, and he doesn't get to have that. He doesn't get to see that he broke me. I listened to my heart, and I only have myself to blame. I walk to the doorway and look at him. "Take your shit and get out of my house." I walk right past him toward the front door. Every single step, I feel my body get heavier and heavier. I open the door, and Quinn is right there to catch me before I fall.

"I got you," he says. My eyes just close, and I see black.

"Bring her in the house." I hear Asher's voice, the anguish in his tone. "I'm leaving." I hear his footsteps get farther and farther away from me. The sound of the truck door closing and leaving makes my eyes flutter open as I feel myself being carried.

"I think you passed out," Quinn says, and all I can do is close my eyes. "Sorry, but I had to call Chelsea," he says, walking into my bedroom, and I shake my head.

"Couch," I say, and he turns to walk back out to the couch. He places me on the couch, and I look at him.

"He's gone," Quinn says, looking at me and running a hand through his hair, his face white as if he saw a ghost. He walks over to the kitchen and heads straight to where I keep my grandfather's special whiskey. He unscrews the top and takes a huge gulp, his eyes closing as it goes down his throat. I know that burn hurts. "He's …" He shakes his head. "He's destroyed." I'm about to say something, and he holds up his hand. "I'm not on his side," he says right away. "But you didn't see him."

"I don't care." I say the three words that are a lie. I'm a liar just like him. I don't want to think about it. I can't think about it.

The sound of running and the door opening have me looking to the side to see Chelsea there. "What happened?" she asks, rushing over to me, turning to look at Quinn. "Did you get her a cold rag for her to put on her neck?" He shakes his head. "What the fuck have you been doing?" she says, totally unaware of what just went on. "Why are you drinking?"

"It's over." I look at her, and her mouth opens and then closes. "It's a long story."

"It's a fucked-up story," Quinn says from the kitchen, drinking another shot. "It's the story that you never expect to hear, and then you hear it, and you look around wondering, did I just hear what he said." He closes his eyes. "It's like *Twilight Zone* kind of thing."

Chelsea gets up and looks at him like he has two fucking heads. "Asher is Liam's son," I say

the words, and her face turns white. Her mouth opens, then closes again. "Exactly."

"Did he know?" she asks, putting her hand to her stomach, neither of us answering her. So she looks at us again. "Did he know when he came here?" Again we just look at each other and Chelsea sits on the couch next to me. "Does Ethan know?" she asks, and I nod my head.

"I need," I say. "I need to pack his stuff." I turn to get off the couch. "He needs his stuff."

"We need to burn his stuff," Chelsea says, and Quinn laughs.

"Again." He shakes his head when Chelsea gasps out. "Too soon."

"I'm fine." I get up and sit back down when the room spins. Chelsea gets up and holds out her hand. "I'm fine. I just got up too fast," I say, and she doesn't move.

"I'll help you there, and then you can do your thing," she says, and I reach out, taking her hand in mine.

"I feel weird," I say finally. "And I can't explain it," I say, walking with her into my room. "It's almost like …"

"A piece of you is missing," Chelsea says from beside me softly. The tears don't even warn me this time. They just come, one after another, like a dam being opened. My hand covers my mouth to stop the sob. "You don't have to do this," Chelsea says from beside me. "Why don't you do it tomorrow?"

"No," I say, shaking my head. "I need him gone," I say. "I need to see that all of his stuff is gone." She nods her head at me as I go over to the bed and start ripping off the sheets. "These need to go in the garbage." I throw my cover on the floor, followed by the sheets. My body shakes but with rage, rage that I let myself fall for someone who hurt me. Rage that I can't stop thinking about how he is feeling. Rage that all I want to do is ask him to come back. I walk around the bed, grabbing the pillows and also throwing them on the floor.

I don't bother to hide the tears when Quinn comes in. He looks at me and then at Chelsea, who just shakes her head. "Leave her."

"I want it all gone," I tell them both. "I need garbage bags," I say, walking out of the room past both of them and going to the kitchen. Grabbing two from the box, I go back to my room. "Quinn, hold the bag open, and I'll throw the stuff in it." I shake the garbage bag open. "Chelsea, help me put the stuff in the bag," I say, and she helps me with no questions asked. I grab the other bag and walk around the room, throwing out everything that reminds me of him.

Picking up the little glass jar that he bought me last week with the two little red roses in them, I throw it into the empty garbage bag, the sound of the glass shattering makes me look up. "It's funny," I say, looking down at the bag, then up again. "I thought when my heart broke earlier, I would hear it shatter, just like the glass did." I wipe my cheek when Chelsea takes a step forward, and I hold up my hand. "I just want all of his stuff gone so I never have to look at it again," I say, my voice going lower. "The sooner I do that, the sooner I can forget about him."

Thirty-One

Asher

I WAIT FOR Quinn to come out of the house, carrying two huge garbage bags. He walks right over to me. "Here," he says, dropping the bags at my feet.

"What are those?" I ask, looking down at the two bags.

"The bedding and some stuff she didn't want," he says, and if my heart wasn't shattered before, it's definitely shattered now.

"How is she doing?" I ask, looking back at the house and seeing that all the lights are off.

"She went from laughing to crying to throwing shit," he answers honestly. "Chelsea put something in her tea."

"Fuck." I shake my head. "Is Chelsea staying?" I ask and then hear a car coming. Looking up I see that it's

Mayson. He gets out of the truck, opening the door in the back and grabbing a bag out of it.

He comes over to us. "Figured you would still be here," he says. "Are you going anywhere?"

"As long as Liam is out there, I'm not going anywhere," I say, and he nods at me. "I'll be out here if you need me."

"Why don't you go to my place?" Mayson says. "I don't know how she is going to react if she sees you here."

"I can't leave her," I say, looking at them. "What would you do?" They both share a look. "Would you leave Willow?" I ask Quinn.

"I didn't even know her name, and I wouldn't leave her," Quinn says, folding his arms over his chest.

"And you," I say to Mayson. "Would you leave Chelsea?"

"Not in this lifetime," he says. "But …" he says, and I say something, and he holds up his hand. "Hear me out. If she comes out here and sees you're here, it might push her over the edge, and she might never come back."

"He's right," Quinn says. "And I never say Mayson is right. It actually physically pains me to say he's right."

"I don't want to hurt her," I say, and they both get it. "What if she wants to see me and I'm not here?"

"Then I'll call you, and you can get here in under four minutes," Mayson says and tosses me his keys. "Go, and I swear if anything, and I mean anything, happens, I'll call you."

"I can't go," I tell them the truth. "I just can't."

"At least hide the truck," he says, and I nod at him. Quinn turns and goes to his truck and leaves, and I pack the two bags into the truck.

I spend the night watching the house, wondering if she is okay. I spend the night sitting on the porch, hoping I can get a glimpse of her if she wakes up. When the sun comes up, the front door opens, and I spring out of my chair, my heart beating out of my chest and my hand itching to hold her.

The door opens, and Chelsea comes out with two cups of coffee in her hand. "Figured you would still be here," she says, handing me a cup.

"How is she?" I ask, looking over her shoulder, hoping to see her. Hoping to talk to her and tell her how sorry I am. Hoping like fuck she can forgive me somehow.

"She just went to bed," she says. "She was up all night looking at the ceiling in her bedroom, and then she decided she didn't want to sleep in her bed. So she got up and tried to sleep on the couch and then didn't want to lie there." She takes a sip of her coffee. "I've never seen her like this. She's usually the strong one." The burning in my stomach starts to form.

"The last thing I want to do is hurt her," I tell Chelsea, and she smiles at me sadly.

"I don't know how you are going to make her forgive you," she answers me honestly. "But if it matters, I'm rooting for you." I smile sadly. "Not for you but for her. She deserves to be happy. She deserves to have a man by her side who isn't going to fuck her over. She deserves for someone to carry her burden for once and not that she carries it on her own."

The lump in my throat forms again, and I know that I'm that man. I'm the man she needs. I want to be that man for her. I would do anything for her. "I'll die fighting," I say, handing her back the coffee. "I have to go, but I'll be back."

"We got her," she says, and her words hurt me more than I can describe, more than I can say.

I make a pit stop before heading to Jacob's house. Pulling up at the barn, I can see the light on inside, and I know he's already here. I get out of the truck, and the tightness in my neck is just as bad as the tightness in my stomach.

He walks out of the barn with a cup of coffee in his hand. His jeans and plaid shirt are like a uniform with his cowboy hat.

"Hey, Billy," I say, and I can see from the way he looks at me that he knows. "I was wondering if you had a minute," I say, and he just nods his head. "I'm sorry," I tell him, "for not being honest with you about who I was."

"You had your reasons," Billy says, bringing the cup to his mouth. "Knew you were hiding something." My eyes search his. "Knew the minute I looked in your eyes. I just didn't know what it was."

"I should have just come out and told you right away," I admit. "You guys accepted me and gave me more than anyone has ever given to me, and I should have done things differently."

"I knew you would tell me eventually." He smirks. "I

didn't think it would be this." He takes a sip of his coffee.

"Go big or go home," I joke with him and shake my head.

"You're a good man, Asher," he tells me. "Regardless of who shares your blood."

"Thank you," I tell him. "Coming from you, it means everything. She'll never forgive me." I wait now, and he takes a deep breath.

"I reckon with time she will," he says, but his tone is not convincing. "She didn't shoot you. That's a good sign."

I shake my head now, knowing I needed this moment right here. "Thank you," I say. "I don't think I could ever repay you."

"Make it right with her, and we can call it even." He turns now and walks back into the barn, leaving me looking up at the sky.

"I'll die trying," I say to myself.

I get in the truck and make my way over to Jacob's house. Ethan is already there sitting on the step, waiting. He gets up when he sees my truck and walks over to me. "You look like shit, brother," he says, and I stop and look at him. "My dad is coming, but um …" he says, and the door opens, and Kallie comes out. I can see that she spent the night pretty much crying because her eyes are puffy and red, and it kills me to know I did that to her. I did it to her daughter. She comes down the stairs with Jacob beside her. "Brace yourself."

I brace myself for the slap that is going to come. I brace myself for the harsh and vicious words. I brace myself for the wrath of a mother. I'm waiting for it to happen, and she just walks up to me and slowly hugs me. "I'm so so sorry," she whispers and tries not to cry. "No one deserves what happened to you." I'm shocked by her reaction. Not used to anyone caring about me.

I look over at Ethan and Jacob, who just rubs her back. "He's fine," Jacob says to her. "Look, he's healthy and strong."

She lets me go. "I'm sorry for getting your shirt wet."

"It's fine," I say softly.

"We have to go, Mom, or else we'll get back late," Ethan says, opening the back of the truck and getting in.

"Did you sleep last night?" Jacob asks, and I shake my head. "Looks like I'm driving," he says, turning to Kallie. "I'll see you later."

I'm turning to get into the truck when I hear the sound of another car. I look up to see Beau arriving. He gets out of his car and comes over to us. "Sorry I'm late," he says, and I just look at him. "Why do you look surprised that I'm here?"

"I just figured," I say, and he slaps my shoulder with his hand, and he squeezes. "I lied to you guys, and you'd want me gone?"

"We owe you more than you know," Beau says. "My brother doesn't know his ass from his elbow, but know that from this day on, you have family." He smiles at me. "We take care of our own."

I don't say anything to him. Instead, I just nod and walk to the back of the truck. Jacob and Beau get into the truck, and I look out the window. A lone tear runs down my cheek as I watch Kallie wave goodbye.

When we arrive at the bank, Jacob looks around to make sure that nothing seems out of the norm. We walk into the bank, and the girl at the counter smiles at me. "How can I help you?"

"I have a safety-deposit box here I'd like to get into," I say, and she asks for my name and then tells me it will just be a minute. She comes back and tells us to follow her. My whole body feels numb. This whole thing is something out of a movie, yet it's my real life. I step into the room with her, walking to the wall of boxes. She sticks her key in mine, and I take the key out and turn. The long beige box comes out, almost like Pandora's box. She points me over to a room with a table and four chairs.

Placing the box on the table, I flip the lid open, and the only thing in there is the envelope. When Ethan sees it, he pulls out a chair and sits down. "Just seeing it again," he says. "Fucks with my head."

Jacob stands next to him. "He doesn't have the power," he tells him, and I take the envelope out and hand it to Beau.

He pulls the letter out that I got. "Is this like yours?" he asks Ethan, and he just scans it and then nods. "I mean, mine said my parents were liars. You didn't get that part." He continues to read it.

"What else is in there?" Beau asks, and he opens the letter and looks at the paper and gasps out. The three of us just look at him.

"Holy fuck," he says and then looks at me. "Did you

read this?" He holds up the paper, and I just shake my head.

"It was all a blur. There was the DNA proof and all that, and I didn't really look at that one. Why?"

"Because according to this paper." He reads it. "You are rightfully heir to his money as soon as you turn thirty." I look at him, confused. "Liam's allowance will be stopped as soon as you turn thirty."

"Oh my God," Jacob says, looking at the paper.

"And if you are not around to collect it," he continues, "Liam's allowance will continue as usual."

"What about Ethan?" I ask, looking at him, hoping he doesn't feel left out.

"Ethan gets control after Liam dies." He laughs. "Apparently, I've got my inheritances, which is the mayor's office." He shakes his head. "What a fucking idiot." He continues to read the paper "You're loaded," Beau says. "Really loaded." He flips over the papers.

"We need to make sure that nothing happens to these papers," Jacob says, and Beau puts the papers on the desk and takes pictures of them and then emails them to Casey.

Who calls him right away. "What is this?" he asks.

"That is the whole reason Liam is trying to get rid of Asher," Beau says and fills him in.

"I'm going to send this to my lawyer and make sure it's filed with the court," Casey says. "He's going to make sure that everything is put into place."

I sit at the table, not knowing what the hell is going on. My head spins around and around. "I don't understand any of this," I admit, and Beau smiles.

"For once, the good guy is going to win," he says, turning his attention back to the phone.

"I had everything I ever wanted or needed," I admit. "I had a woman who I loved with everything I had and who loved me back." I shake my head, the pain of not seeing her today too much to bear. "I had a job I loved. I was finally fucking happy. The money meant fucking nothing to me."

"And then it's ripped away from you, and all you can do is watch it slip away," Ethan says, his hand going to my arm. "You are going to get her back," he says, but even I know how Amelia is. I know how stuck in her ways she is. If she has written me off, I'm written off, and nothing anyone can say or do will change her mind.

"If Liam is looking for me," I say. "I won't stay here and wait for him like a sitting duck." I swallow, knowing what I have to do. "I have to leave and go as far away from you guys as I can go."

"Or," Ethan says, looking at Jacob. "We lead him to us."

Here, in the middle of a bank, the four of us put together a plan that I can either walk out alive or walk out dead.

Thirty-Two

AMELIA

I OPEN MY eyes and look over, seeing the bed empty. The pain in my chest comes right away as I turn away from what was his spot. The tear runs down my face, no matter how much I fight it. I finally sent everyone home last night. It's been three days of everyone hovering around me, and I needed space.

I flip the covers off me and get up, my body aching. Grabbing my robe, I walk out to the coffee maker. Looking outside, I find the sky starting to turn a little gray with the sun coming up. It's been three days since I've seen him. It's been three days since I felt his touch. It's been three days since I could breathe without feeling like something was lodged in my chest.

When it's the quietest is when it's the worst. It's

when my mind has time to wander. It's when my mind plays games with me and makes me remember the little things. When he used to kiss me right behind my ear and say I love you. When he used to bring me coffee in the morning. When he would make me feel like I've never felt before. It's all there, no matter how much I try to put it in a box and lock it. I pour the black coffee into the mug and turn to drink it in the kitchen. Even my house isn't a sacred place anymore. Every single corner has a memory of him. I blink away the stinging of the tears that threaten to come.

The soft knock on the door makes me shake my head. I walk over, wondering which family member could be here so early. I don't even check, and when I open the door, my body tenses up while my heart starts to beat for the first time in three days without pain. "Asher." His name falls off my lips in a whisper.

"I know you don't want me here," he says, and I take a second while he is talking to look at him. He is wearing blue jeans and a white shirt, nothing he hasn't worn before, but it feels like home to me. His eyes are red, and it looks like he hasn't slept in three days. His face is covered with a beard, and his brown eyes have no shine in them. No light. "I just need five minutes of your time, and then I'll be gone." He looks at me, and my hand doesn't move from the door handle as I grip it with everything in me to stay in place. "I'm leaving town," he says the three words that I was hoping to hear, yet make the pain in my chest feel like someone is setting my body on fire. It's a pain I've never felt before. A pain that goes deep to your bones. "I tried to stay, and I made reasons for staying, but it's just too much," he says, his voice almost breaking as he looks down and sniffles. "Not being able to be with you or see you. I just … there is no reason for me to stay." My tongue feels like it's a hundred pounds. "But I wanted to let you know that what happened between us was nothing that I planned. Falling in love with you."

"Was a lie," I finally say, and if he didn't look like he was in pain before, I know my words cut him.

"Nothing about how I felt for you was a lie. Nothing about what we shared was a lie." He shakes his head. "What I felt for you was the most real thing I've ever felt. What I felt for you …" His eyes fill with tears, and a smile fills his face. "What I felt for you will never go away. It will stay with me until the day I die. You, Amelia McIntyre, will forever be the love of my life." My hands shake. "I hope you find someone who can give you everything you deserve," he says, turning and walking down the steps. He turns back one last time. "I love you, Amelia." The tears run down his face. "Until my last dying breath, I'll love you." He takes one last look at me and turns around to walk back to his truck.

My feet don't move from the spot even after the red lights from his truck disappear in the distance. The tears continue rolling down my face, one after another. When my hand finally lets go of the door handle, I shut the door softly.

The shower helps wash away the tears, and when I walk into the barn forty-five minutes later, my grandfather is there waiting for me. I look at him, shocked when he walks over to me. "What are you doing here?" I ask.

"Was wondering if you had time to take a ride with your grandfather," he says, and I see that my horse is there and saddled already. "Figured you needed to clear your head."

I swallow, nodding, and walk to my horse with his arms around my shoulders. I put my foot in the stirrup and push myself up. We ride side by side down the path he used to take me when I was a little girl. "I remember when I used to take you down this path." My grandfather starts talking. "And you wouldn't stop talking. You would talk about the air and the trees." I smile at him. "It was the part I enjoyed most," he says softly. "So what's on your mind?" he asks, and when I look over at him, I can't help but cry. "Might as well get it all out."

"Nothing really," I say as he stops our horses when we get closer to the creek. He gets off his horse, and I follow, getting off mine. He grabs the reins to both horses and leads them to the water.

"Let's go sit down," he says, pointing at the rock where I used to sit on when I was younger. I sit down and look over at the tree where my parents engraved their name. He sits next to me as we watch the creek move along. "When I found out that you and Tex were a couple," he starts, and I look at him shocked. "You think I didn't know." He shakes his head. "I knew about it. I also knew there was something about him that I didn't like."

"Well, you should have shared the information with

me," I say, and he laughs.

"Would you have listened?" he asks, and it's my turn to laugh. "Exactly.

"Life is all about mistakes," he says, and I bring my legs up and hug them to my chest. I put my head on my knees as I watch him talk. "Everyone makes them."

"He lied to me, Grandpa," I say, the tears are running down and soaking through my pants.

"Did he?" he asks, and I huff out. "He isn't Tex."

My mouth opens. "It's the same thing," I point out. "Omitting to tell me who he was is just as bad as Tex showing up at my birthday party with his wife. Even when I say the words, I know it's not the same. I know deep down it's not the same, but the fact that he hid it from me. The fact that he wasn't truthful. That he lied about who he was."

"Did you ever think about how he must feel?" he asks. "Knowing that you have a family out there after being alone all your life. Knowing that your father just left your mother and you like you were trash."

"He isn't trash," I finally say. "He's …" My voice trails off.

"Your father lied to your mother," he says, and my head comes up. "All those years ago, he lied to her about being Ethan's father." My mouth opens, and he holds up his hand. "He's Ethan's father, there is no mistake about it, just as I'm Ethan's grandfather and I would fight anyone who says otherwise. I love him just as much as I love all of you." He smiles and puts his big hand on my cheek. "But your father made a mistake and lied. What if your mother never forgave him?" He tilts his head, and I see the side of his eyes crinkle when he smiles. "I don't even want to think of it."

"Me either," I answer him right away.

"A man steps up when he's wrong and admits that he fucked up," he says, and I laugh because he curses so infrequently. "He messed up, honey, and he knows it."

"I don't know if I can forgive him." The truth comes out. "What if I say I do, and I throw it in his face?"

He throws his head back. "You know damn straight you are going to do that regardless. Your grandmother still throws things I did to her when I was seventeen." He looks down. "Can you imagine your life without him?" I don't answer him. "All you have to think about is how will you feel knowing someone out there will be holding his hand?" The thought makes me sick. "How will you feel knowing someone else is going to love him? If that doesn't bother you, then let him go." I put my chin on my knees and look at the creek.

Neither of us says anything when we hear a blaring sound of an alarm filling the forest. My grandfather's phone rings and so does mine. "Someone has broken into the utility barn," my grandfather says.

And at the exact same time, I yell out, "Asher!"

Thirty-Three

ASHER

I PULL INTO the barn parking lot and let out the biggest sigh. I wrap my arms around the steering wheel and place my head on it. Walking away from her for the second time destroyed me. I didn't think I could do it. I wanted to beg and plead for her to take me back. I wanted to promise never to lie to her again. I wanted to do all of that, but I knew I couldn't. I knew I couldn't drag her into this mess with Liam. Until we know where he is, I am staying clear of her.

Pushing off, I head toward the barn. It's where I've been staying the past couple of days. Beau fought with me and so did Jacob and Ethan, but I couldn't take them up on their offer. I also didn't want Amelia to feel like they chose me over her.

I open the door to step into the barn, turning to turn the alarm off. I stop dead in my tracks when I see the alarm is already off. I turn around, looking into the dark barn, and the only light is coming in from the open door. "Hello?" I say, flipping the switch and seeing that none of the lights turn on. I take two steps into the barn, and I know someone is here. "Hello?" I call out again and walk a couple of steps in. The light from the top window gives a little light in the middle of the barn. Bales of hay are all around me. I stand in the middle of the room, looking in each corner, when I see a shadow on the right. I watch him walk toward me, the hair on the back of my neck sticks up when I see him finally in the light. "Who are you?" I ask the man who stands there wearing a linen suit. His black hair pushed back with the front strands falling onto his forehead.

"Well, well, well," he says once he's close enough. "If it isn't the son I never knew about," he says. I feel physically ill when he gets close enough, and I smell the aftershave he wears. "Got to say …" He shakes his head. "I did good with you."

"I am not your son," I say, my hands balled into fists at my sides.

He laughs, and everything from my blood to my bones goes cold. "With that attitude, you definitely are my son." I stand where I am, hoping I'm not here alone. Hoping someone is out there with me. "Your mother …" he starts. "I met her when I was on my way home." He looks up and puts his hands on his hips. "She was so hard to get into bed." I want to throat punch him, but instead,

I let him talk. "But when I did, fuck, did she light up."

I swallow the bile that comes up my throat. "I would come home and go back for her. That is how good she was. When she told me she was pregnant, I laughed at her. Like I would take her word that I was the father. From what I saw, she gave it away to everyone." He shakes his head. "She wasn't stupid, that is for sure. One night, the bitch followed me home. She rang my doorbell and pounded on the door, ranting and yelling that she was pregnant with my child. My mother took her in, and the next morning, my father dropped her off. She took five thousand dollars from them and told them she would get rid of you." He shakes his head.

"Guess she lied about that," I say. "I'm standing right in front of you."

"I should have made sure she went to the doctor. But by then, I was working my way into Savannah's bed." He mentions Ethan's mother.

"Your father paid off that situation also, didn't he?" I look at him.

"My father was always so fucking charitable." The tone coming out of him is as if his father was so stupid.

"Not that charitable." I finally find the words. "Considering that in a month, I'll be getting all of his money, and you'll be stuck with nothing." The color leaves his face. I clap my hands and laugh. "Imagine that, the son of a bitch is getting everything." I take a step toward him. "And you are getting nothing," I hiss.

"That fucking money is mine!" he roars out. "It's all mine. It was me who had to swallow all the shit he threw at me. I had to swallow my tongue every fucking time just to please him. Even when he fucked my wife," he says between clenched teeth. "But no more. I am not going to take anything anymore. And I'm not going to have you step between me and what I deserve."

"Is that why you burned down the barn?" I ask, and his eyes shine as if he is proud of it.

"You aren't as stupid as I thought you were," he says, a smile filling his face. "Burning the barn was for two reasons. One was a warning for you to leave." He smirks. "Two was because I could."

"What were you going to achieve by burning down the barn?" I ask him. "It wasn't even mine. I wasn't even there."

"Exactly, but you're here," he says. "I knew the minute I told that fine piece of ass that I was in town, you would be out on your ass and no one would be protecting you." He sneers at me. "I thought for sure when I hired that fucker to knock her out, you would have left. But did you leave? No, not my son. Why do I have to have sons who protect their women?" I lunge forward, surprising him, and grab the collar of his jacket, yanking him to me so his face is right in front of mine.

"If you fucking touch her," I hiss in his face, my nose almost touching his, "I'll kill you with my bare hands."

"Asher." I hear Jacob walk into the barn taking in the scene. "Don't do it."

"Oh, look who it is," Liam says, and I let him go. He steps back, smoothing down the front of his jacket. "The other shmuck who got stuck raising my kid."

"You're a fucking waste," I say. "Your father was right about you." I look at him. "What was it that he put in the letter he gave me?" I take a second to remember it. "You're pathetic and a swine, nothing like a real man should be." I know the words hit right in the chest. "Nothing like he was. Nothing like he raised you to be. Instead, you were the pussy of the family." I shake my head. "Did you get it?"

"Yeah." Jacob nods his head.

"Get what?" Liam asks, his hair falling more and more in his face.

"Your confession," I say. "You were so eager to tell me how you planned to fuck me over." I shake my head. "Forget that you were stupid enough to light the match to burn down the barn and then smoke a cigarette, leaving your DNA at the scene." I laugh at how pathetic he is. "And the fact we found the money wire from you to the man you hired to take out Amelia. The fact that you cut the wires to the alarm system at this barn. Oh, and let's not forget the motel room you've been renting out for the last month." He looks like he's seen a ghost. "Little did you know that we've been on to you for the last three days. You see what you did wrong there, dear old Dad?" I say. "You showed your hand too soon. Thought your three of a kind would win. What you didn't know was I had the full fucking house." I open my arms to my sides and laugh at him. "You did all that, and in the end, I. Still. Fucking. Win." I look him straight in the eye when I say the next line, the sound of sirens off in the distance. "And. You. Fucking. Lose." He reaches behind his back, and I see the gun come out as he aims it at me.

"Asher!" I hear yelled right before the sound of the shot rings out.

Thirty-Four

Amelia

THE RIDE BACK to the barn takes forever, or at least I think it takes forever. The sound of sirens off in the distance makes my whole body go stiff. "Leave the horse." Willow rushes out of the barn when we get back. "And go. Quinn is already on his way there, and we are locking down the barn," she says, and I look over to see all the other workers starting to close everything down.

I get off my horse. My grandfather is already five steps ahead of me, running to my car. He starts the car when the phone rings in his hand. "You're on speakerphone. I'm on my way," he says right away.

"Dad, do not come here," my uncle Casey says, and I can hear sirens coming from his phone along with the sound of him running.

"I'm with Amelia," he tells him, and my uncle groans.

"We're closed off," he tells him. "They aren't letting anyone in." My heart sinks.

"What's happening?" I ask, and he stops running.

"Someone said they heard a gunshot." The minute he says the word, my eyes close. "I can't confirm it yet, but we have the EMTs coming."

"She isn't going to sit at home," my grandfather says, and we pull up as close as we can. I open the door before he even has a chance to say goodbye. The sheriff's truck is stopping anyone from getting any closer to the barn. My eyes go to the barn as I spot Asher's truck parked there with four other trucks surrounding him. Men are running in and out of the barn. People are everywhere. An EMT truck is there with the lights on as they run into the barn.

"I need to get there," I say to the man who I've met a couple of times when I went to visit my father at his office.

"I'm sorry. I've been told to block everyone from getting closer," he says, and I look behind me as the EMT truck comes straight toward us. I move to the side of the deputy's truck while the EMT drives around him. He is going too fast for it to be nothing. I put my hand over my eyes to look without the sun blinding me.

My breaths come in pants as my mouth waters, and I think I'm going to be sick on the side of the road. "Oh my God," I say, putting my hand on my forehead. My feet move as I pace in front of him. "Oh my God." I stop moving and put my hands on my knees as I start to panic. He walked away from me thinking I didn't love him goes through my head. The last thing I said to him was it was a lie. "Oh my God," I say, trying to catch my breath. My grandfather rubs my back.

"Breathe in and out," he says. "Focus and breathe." I listen to him and then turn to the deputy, shaking my head.

"I have to get in there." He looks at me and then looks back at the barn. "My father is in there," I say, pushing past him, and he knows better than to follow me. I hear my grandfather issuing an apology and saying that it's going to be okay. I run to the entrance of the barn.

Another deputy is there, stopping me from going closer as he talks on his radio. "You need to stay out here."

"What's going on?" I ask, hoping he tells me that this is just a precaution. Hoping he tells me it's nothing. Hoping like hell the beating of my heart echoing in my ears will let me listen to what he has to say. My mouth goes dry and my hands start to shake as I look at the second ambulance take their stretcher out.

"One person shot," he says, and my hand goes to my mouth. "Not sure he's going to make it."

"Oh my God." I push past him as I'm walking toward the barn. The tears run down my face, and I see the ambulance come out with a man on it, his black hair stopping me from moving.

My legs give out on me, and I hit the grass with his name on my lips. The sob rips through me, and all I can do is put my hands on my chest. "Asher," I say softly. People walk in and out of the barn, and it's almost like a dream when I see him walking out.

He's looking down, and his white shirt has blood on it. I get up. "Asher." I call out his name, and he looks up. His eyes find mine, and he runs over to me. I meet him halfway. He wraps his arms around me, and I smell him while I sob. I wrap my arms around his neck, and he picks me up around my waist. "I'm sorry," I whisper in his ear. "I'm so, so sorry." I let go of him and kiss his lips. "I don't care what your name is," I say between wiping my face with the back of my hand. He leans in and kisses me softly. "I know in my heart who you are," I say. "You're okay." My hands go to his face to touch him. To make sure this isn't a dream. "Are you hurt?"

"No." He places me down on my feet and looks down at me. He reaches his hand up to cup my face. I turn my face and kiss his palm.

"I thought you were shot," I say softly, and I see my father coming to us followed by Ethan, Casey, Quinn, and Beau. "How did they get here so fast?" I ask.

"You were supposed to make sure she stayed away from here," my father says, looking over my head to my grandfather, standing with his hands on his hips.

"You had one job," my uncle Casey says, shaking his head.

"Nice, Grandpa," Quinn says, smirking at him.

"You guys think you can stop her?" my grandfather says. "You also said everything would be okay." He puts out his hands.

"It was," Beau says, shaking his head.

"Does this look like everything is okay?" My grandfather takes off his cowboy hat and holds it in one hand as he holds both hands out at his sides. "Two ambulances. Five police cars."

"It was a precaution," Ethan says. "We had it under control."

"Wait, what?" I say, stepping away from Asher but not far enough that I can't feel him next to me. "What am I missing?" I look around at all the men, none of them looking directly at me. "What is going on?"

"I'm out," Quinn says. "My phone is blowing up."

"Before we tell you." My father looks at me. "We did it to protect you."

Ethan laughs at him and puts his hand on his shoulder. "Dad, you've been using that line forever." He shakes his head. "Also, it never works."

"If you guys don't mind," Asher says, "I'd like to tell her myself. Plus, you have some paperwork to do." He points at the ambulance. "Are you going to make sure he's okay?" He turns to Beau.

"Nope." He shakes his head. "He made his bed, so let him lie in it."

He grabs my hand and walks over to his truck. "Asher." My father calls his name, and he turns around. "Told you that you had it in you." He smiles and turns to walk to the ambulance.

He puts me in the truck and leans in to kiss me. My hand comes up to touch his cheek. "We really have to talk."

I nod my head, not saying anything as the tears come. "Let's go home," I say, and he closes the door. We don't say anything on the drive to my house, but I don't let his hand leave my lap the whole time.

When we finally walk into the house, he closes the door behind him. "Do you want some water?" I ask, nervous and scared that he's going to decide that maybe I'm not the person for him. Maybe me giving him up so easily shows him I won't stand by his side. I look at him, wiping the tears rolling out of my eyes. "I know that what I did was wrong," I say. "And I know that I should have given you a chance to talk but …"

"It hurt you," he says for me. "I hurt you, and you have to know I never, ever wanted to not tell you. I just." He takes a deep breath. "I just didn't know how. Look, I was never going to stay." He swallows. "I wanted to come and meet Ethan. I just wondered how he grew up. I wondered if he grew up like me, but when I saw it was night and day, I was glad." I take a step forward, and he shakes his head. "If you come any closer, I'll forget everything I have to tell you. There were things I found out a couple of days ago I didn't even know."

"Whatever it is," I say. "It doesn't matter."

"No," he says. "I'm not keeping anything from you. The day after I told Jacob and Ethan about it, we rode to the bank, and I showed them the papers and letters I got. I didn't even read it all, but Beau did, and everything clicked into place. Liam was living on an allowance, which was going to end once I turn thirty. It took Casey a couple of hours to find out he was in debt up to his ass.

He owed everyone money, and soon, it was running out unless he got rid of me." I gasp out. "We knew he was getting desperate, so it was a matter of time before he did something stupid. We've been following him for the past couple days. We knew today would be the day. He was staying at the motel in town. Ethan had followed him to the barn. Jacob was on standby. The minute he cut the alarm wires, we knew."

"You came here this morning," I say. "To say goodbye to me."

His eyes stare into mine. "Anything could have happened. I wanted you to know that I loved you." I try to block the sob that comes out with my hand. He comes over to me, holding my face in his hand. "I wanted you to know that I love you with everything that I have." My hands go to his chest as I feel his heart beating underneath. "Six months ago, I had forty-seven cents to my name. Next month, I'll have five point seven million dollars."

My mouth opens in shock and then closes. "You could have nothing, and I would still love you," I say. "The thought of losing you." I swallow the huge lump, I close my eyes and the tears run over. "I don't ever want to feel that again. I won't survive," I say the truth. "Losing you would be like losing me."

"You won't lose me," he says. "Unless Liam put a bullet in me, I was coming back to fight for you." He wipes a tear away. "I was going to fight for us, and I wasn't taking no for an answer." His hand goes around my waist, and he picks me up. "Now, let's go take a shower. I haven't touched you in over four days, so I have a lot of catching up to do." I don't say anything to him. I let him carry me to the bathroom, and I savor every single second of it.

Epilogue One

ASHER

Six months later

"MR. ASHER NORMAND." The man on stage calls me, and I walk up the four stairs toward him. He holds out his hand for me to shake and holds what I've been working toward. I smile at the guy and then look out into the crowd.

The cheers are so loud it's making me blush. "You're a popular guy, Mr. Normand," he says.

"My family takes it a bit overboard," I say, shaking my head as I walk down off the stage and toward my seat. My foot moves up and down as I wait until the end of the ceremony before I can get up.

Amelia is the first one I see as she gets on her tippy-toes and kisses me. "Congratulations, officer."

"Stop hoggin' him," Ethan says, pushing her aside. "There he is, my big brother." I laugh at him as he hugs me. "I've never had a big brother. It's also gross you're dating my sister." He fake vomits, and I push his shoulder. Since we found out that we have the same father and are half brothers, he's become my best friend. I have to wonder if we would be best friends regardless.

"We are so proud of you," Kallie says with tears in her eyes. She has stepped up and welcomes me with open arm. She treats me exactly as a son. I turn and see Jacob with his own tears in his eyes.

"I knew you could do it," he says to me when I walk to him, and he hugs me. "Proud of you, son." I hug him, my own tears coming to my eyes. He has taken me under his wing and has been the father I've never had. Beau has been the shining light and has been there for me every time I've needed him. And with my father in jail and fighting everything, I've needed him. He got life in jail for all of his crimes, and little did we know we were just scratching the surface. They also found out that he burned two of his houses down, committing insurance fraud.

"Can I have my guy back, please?" Amelia says, and I shake my head. "Besides, we have to get home and celebrate," she says. "Everyone is waiting at the bar."

"Okay, I have to stop at home and get Emily and the kids," Ethan says, walking out. "They made Uncle Asher a card."

"Don't forget my girl," I say, and he groans out.

"Stay away from my daughter." He points at me. "Last time, she didn't even want to let you go."

"She's got great taste." Amelia wraps her arms around my waist. "But she better keep her mitts off my man."

"She's three," Ethan says, laughing as he gets into his truck.

We get into the truck with Jacob and Kallie and make our way over to the bar. The parking lot is already full.

"This better not be for me." I glare over at Amelia, who just shakes her head.

"It's a going-away party for Reed, too," she says. "I can't believe he's leaving tomorrow."

"Another family member joining the military," Jacob says. "Casey is going to go nuts."

"Olivia might enlist with him," Kallie says of Reed's mother.

We get out and walk into the bar, and everyone cheers. I raise my hand and walk in, shaking people's hands until I get to Billy, who just shakes his head with his hands on his hips. "Well, I guess you quit." His eyes glisten with tears as he hugs me.

"Nah," I say. "I'll work there on my days off." I put my hand on his shoulder.

"I want grandbabies," he says, looking at me.

"Hey, he can't have the cow for free," Charlotte says. "He's got to put a ring on that finger."

I don't say anything as I look over at Amelia, who is on the side talking to one of our newer waitresses, Hazel.

The crowd cheers again, and I look over to see Reed entering, followed by Christopher and his parents.

"Thank you," he says. "Drinks are on me."

"Idiot." I hear Amelia from the side. "Like he has any money to pay for drinks."

"I got it covered, baby," I say, and she smiles up at me and kisses me.

The night flies by with both of us busy behind the bar. The only difference is I can kiss her when I want. "Okay, big boy, time for you to go," Amelia says to Reed, who is sitting on a stool at the bar. Everyone else has left.

"Where the hell is Hazel?" Reed says, and you can tell he's had a couple of whiskeys. The two of them have been getting closer since she started even though they've known each other their whole lives.

"She took the night off," Amelia says, and I look over at her, knowing full well Hazel was here. "Besides, it was just family and friends tonight, so I didn't think we needed her."

I look over at him and can see he's a little bit disappointed by this news. He taps his finger on the bar. "Okay, I'm out. See you all tomorrow." He turns and walks out of the bar.

"Who are you all?" Amelia says, shaking her head.

"Is it just us?" I look at her, and she smiles at me. I walk around the bar and lock the front door.

"Closed," I say and walk toward her. I hold out my hand. "Dance with me." I pull her to the dance floor, going onto the stage and plugging my phone in, the song playing right away.

She waits for me in the middle of the dance floor. Her smile is still the best thing I've ever seen. "Our song," she says, putting her arms around my shoulders. "I love you," she says, and I look down at her, and I kiss her lips.

"I love you," I say, my heart starting to beat uncontrollably, and my palms get suddenly sweaty. "You know that, right?"

She laughs. "I figured it out."

"Loving you," I say, "was the easiest thing I've ever done. It just came so naturally to me." I move away from her and reach into my pocket to pull out the diamond ring I've been carrying around all day. I get down on one knee. "I was going to do this six months ago," I say. "The minute I walked out of that barn and saw you on your knees, I knew I wanted to spend the rest of my life with you." I smirk. "I mean, I knew way before then, but seeing you there just cemented it." She puts her hands to her mouth. "I also knew before then that I couldn't do it without being someone," I say as the tear comes to my eye.

She grabs my face. "You are someone," she says, kissing my lips. "You are everything."

"I wanted you to be proud to have my last name. I wanted to be sure I had something to give you," I say honestly. "I want to hold your hand and kiss you good night. I want to dry your tears when you get sad. I want to watch you carry our babies and be the best mother in the world. Every single memory that I have, I want it to be with you by my side." I look into her gorgeous blue eyes. "So, Amelia McIntyre …" She sobs out. "Will you be my wife?" She nods her head and holds out her hand for me to slip the ring on.

She gasps when she sees it. "Is this …?"

"Billy gave it to me tonight," I say. "Said he's been waiting for me to say something." She looks at the ring. "I asked him for your hand." Her mouth opens. "I mean, after your father and your mother. And your brother."

"You, Asher Normand, are my everything." I bend and finally kiss my future wife.

SOUTHERN SECRETS SOUTHERN

Epilogue Two
AMELIA

Six years later

"SIT RIGHT HERE," I tell our two-year-old son as I sit beside him on the stoop of the porch.

"I sit right here, Mommy," he says, looking up at me with his father's face but my eyes. I push the black hair away from his forehead and smile at him. "Right here, Mommy." He swings his little legs. I put my arm around him and bring him to me, kissing his head and smelling the lavender shampoo I used. "Look." He points his finger. "Bird." I look over and then see the white truck coming down the driveway. My son gasps out and looks at me. "Daddy." He claps his hands. He loves me something fierce, but his father … well, he hangs the moon and all the stars.

Asher stops the truck and looks over at us, and just like it did all those years ago, my heart skips a beat. My husband, yeah, being engaged for a week was too much for him and well, he dared my grandfather and father that they couldn't pull off a wedding in a week. News flash: they were done in three, so instead of a barbecue on a Sunday afternoon, we got married. I wore my grandmother's wedding dress and my mother's veil. I slid a gold band on his finger and officially made him mine. He opens the truck door and steps out, wearing his black work boots, cargo pants, and a black deputy's polo. He spent the last six years working his ass off to earn his place in the department.

His aviators hide his brown eyes, but I know they are a light amber when he looks at us. "There they are," he says, putting his glasses on the top of his head and smiling.

"There's my boy," he says, walking to the steps. Our son, JB, gets up, clapping his hands together with glee. The minute he gets to the bottom step, he holds out his hands, and JB jumps into them. Asher's arms catch him, and he buries his face in our son's neck. Our son came screaming into the world at a whopping ten pounds. He was fit to be tied until I fed him, and then he was fine. Asher was adamant about naming our son Jacob Billy, which was a mouthful. And to be honest, I only call him that when I'm really, really mad at him. Otherwise, he is JB to all of us. It wasn't all flowers and roses. Asher doubted he could do it even though I knew he could.

He was just unsure of everything until I left him alone with JB for a couple of hours. "You smell nice," he says, looking over at me. "It's a little early for a bath."

"It was, but he was with Grandpa Billy today for a bit, and well …" I shrug. "They got into trouble, didn't they?"

He looks at our son, trying to hide his smile. "Did you get in trouble?"

"I jumped in the mud," he says without an ounce of remorse. "Grandpa Billy, too."

He shakes his head and looks at me. "You look beautiful," he says, and I glare at him as he leans in and kisses my lips. "Doesn't Mommy look beautiful?"

"Yes," JB says, smiling at me.

He sits next to me, and he puts his arm around me while holding our son on his lap. "Did you have a good day?" I ask and look up when the sound of someone coming down the driveway makes me look up.

I don't have to guess who it is when JB squeals out. My parents stop their truck right next to Asher's. "There he is," my father says, getting out of the truck and coming over. He walks up the two steps, and then JB holds his hands up. "I heard that someone jumped in the mud today."

He nods his head as my father kisses his neck. "Okay, my turn," my mother says and holds out her hands. JB looks at my father and then my mother, not sure who to choose.

"I made cookies," my mother says, and that is all it takes for him to fly into her arms, making us all laugh.

"What are you doing here?" I ask, leaning back on one arm as my hand rubs my big swollen belly.

"You said you didn't sleep last night." My mother looks at me. "So we thought we could take JB home with us."

"I don't know," I say, trying not to smile. "I'm going to miss him a lot."

"It's okay, Mommy," he says. "I'll come back." This kid. I shake my head. "Tomorrow."

"Okay," I huff out. "But you have to be good."

"I will." He holds up his right hand. "I swear."

"We'll just meet you over at the barbecue tomorrow," my father says. "Reed's back," he says, looking down and then looking back up again.

"How is he doing?" I ask.

"Too soon to tell," he says. "Ethan is going to see him later."

"If anyone can understand what he's going through, it's Ethan," Asher says, and it takes my parents five minutes to buckle JB into their truck and drive away.

"What do you say, baby?" Asher says from beside me. "Why don't we go in, and I'll rub your feet?"

"That's how I got into this situation to begin with," I say. "Or was it I just want to fall asleep inside you?" He roars with laughter.

"Hey." He hugs me. "That's our secret." He kisses me.

I shake my head. "You know damn well, Asher Normand, that secrets don't stay secrets for long, especially around us."

Made in the USA
Monee, IL
03 July 2023

38441246R10181